For Z.
A steadfast friend in good times and bad.

Chapter One
Bertram and I Are Engaged

He has even bought me a ring. It is a most unusual one, comprised of a central emerald surrounded by alternating small diamonds and amethysts, and set in white metal. I believe he must have had it designed for me. He muttered something about my uniqueness and worthiness when he pushed it onto my finger after dinner last night. Only Hans and Richenda were present, but Bertram seemed unnecessarily coy about the whole thing. I hope he does not remain embarrassed about my background - or rather what he believes my background to be, for I have yet to tell him the truth. Or is it that, despite my never having confirmed it, he knows I was, for a short time, engaged to Rory? It is not a circumstance I shall ever refer to again, and as Rory is a sensible, if jealous man, I hope he has the good sense to avoid mentioning it himself.

This causes me to wonder if Bertram has yet told Rory that I am officially his betrothed. Rory is currently serving as major-domo at Bertram's water-logged and seemingly doomed estate, White Orchards. Most masters are unlikely to confide in their servants, except perhaps for their valets. The relationship between a gentleman and his valet is one of the most coveted and mysterious of positions. I believe many servants consider it not unlike that of the keeper of the royal chamber for the sovereign. It is the position closest to power in a gentleman's household. And Rory does, on occasion, act as Bertram's valet and is attending to him during his stay at the Muller household, where I am still technically Richenda's paid companion. It is all rather mixed up.

Bertram, Rory, and I have, perforce, often stood on the world stage as equals. We have solved mysteries. We have tried, and failed, to get Bertram and Richenda's elder brother, Richard, rightly convicted of murder and a number of other heinous crimes. Bertram and I were the first to pursue this and affected the one time the man was actually clapped in irons. Then Rory joined the household and being far too clever for his own good - and himself wrongly accused of murder - he became part of our strange trio. All three of us signed a new and very top-secret document called the Official Secrets Act, in which we pledged our lives to the cause of our country and sovereign, should we be called upon to do so. In the past such calls have come from the rather annoying, if thoroughly suave, spy Fitzroy and, frankly, I shall be quite all right if I never see *him* again in all my life.

'Ooh! Look at the colours,' squealed Richenda. The entrée had been removed and, really, the kind of enthusiasm she took in my ring, I have only previously seen her display when anticipating the arrival of pudding.

'It is a most unusual ring,' I said. Bertram had decided to kneel before me to give me the ring - although he had proposed, and I had accepted, some weeks ago. He regarded me with soft brown eyes that looked, for all intents and purposes, like the family's newly acquired spaniel.[1]

'I think it is most lovely,' I said.

'It is the suffragette colours, Euphemia!' exclaimed

---

[1] A gift that Richenda had ordered for her adopted daughter Amy, to distract her from her newly acquired twin baby siblings.

Richenda. 'How glorious it is, obtaining a husband who believes in our struggles.' Whereupon she bit down hard upon a bread roll so as not to display unseemly emotion. (I believe it will be some time before Richenda loses her 'baby weight', if ever.)

Hans, her elegant half-German husband, and my dear friend, stifled a sigh. 'Is it not possible, my dear, that the ring signifies something else? Perhaps a special meaning between them? My own mother's ring spelled out "dearest" in gemstones.'

Hans does not disapprove of equality between men and women, but he has views on how it should be obtained and is still annoyed at Richenda tricking me into a situation where I ended up in the midst of a violent fray, and then in prison...[2]

Bertram rose to his feet and sat down. He glanced at me and I nodded slightly. 'It does have a meaning, but I don't think we are ready to share it yet, are we, dearest?'

I flinched slightly at "dearest", but I signalled my agreement. I knew only too well it was Bertram's way of showing that he believed in women as equals, but neither of us wanted to confirm this to Richenda and start an argument between our hosts.

'How lovely,' said Richenda. Then she sighed and looked down at the substantial diamond engagement ring Hans had given her. She glanced over at her husband reprovingly. Her ring doubtless cost much more than mine, for Hans is a successful banker, but Richenda is always berating him for not being romantic.[3]

---

[2] Please consult my journal *A Death for a Cause*

[3] I rather think Hans could well be romantic, if only she did not so often provoke him.

'When will the wedding be?' asked Hans.

Bertram blushed slightly and tugged at his collar. 'There is still work continuing at the estate, and I am afraid the local church is green with moss and damp. It will be some time before it is suitable for our wedding. Besides, as you may suspect, my brother is determined to throw a spoke in the works if he can.'

'I cannot see how it is anything to do with him,' said Hans. 'If you would consider it, I would be happy to place my estate at your disposal for the wedding. Our village church is most picturesque.'

'Oh, we couldn't possibly,' said Bertram.

Hans smiled gently. 'Allow me this, Bertram. Euphemia has lived under our roof as family and it would be my honour to see her married here.'

This, if ever, was the time to tell them my grandfather was an Earl. My tongue stuck to the roof of my mouth. I had entered Richenda's family's service as a maid when my father died. My mother had been disinherited long ago, for marrying the local curate in a love match that deteriorated into profound unhappiness. When my father died of a heart attack, landing face down in his dish of mutton and onions, my mother, younger brother and I had been left destitute. At the time my mother was no favourite with the local clergy, and we had promptly been given notice to quit the vicarage, hence my decision to enter service in an attempt to support my mother and brother Joe. It was not an option my mother had taken to easily, but even she was forced to admit that we had had little choice. She moved to a rented cottage and terrified the

4

local inhabitants into taking piano lessons.[4]

As I had risen in the ranks of service, so she had become obstinately dedicated on removing me from my occupation. And she knew nothing of the murderous adventures upon which I had become entangled. I could almost fear she was espousing her fiancé, the bishop, purely for my sake, except I was aware that a Prince of the church was the most likely candidate to return her to almost the state of living she had known before she married my poor father. How she had caught her bishop I had no idea, but I suspected a carefully planned campaign.

'We must at least wait until Euphemia's mother has remarried,' said Bertram. 'She is to marry a bishop.'

'Good heavens,' said Richenda. 'A bishop? Your mother has done well for herself. To whom was she previously married? A farmer?'

'A vicar,' I said.

'A most noble profession,' said Hans, giving his wife a warning look.

'But to go from a country girl to living in a bishop's palace. It will be a change for her,' continued Richenda.

'I believe she will comport herself adequately,' I said, while adding internally that she would scare all the local ministry into utter submission within days. My mother, despite her short stature, is a formidable woman, who still remembers fondly causing a Duke to cry during her salad days.

'Of course she will,' said Hans. 'As Euphemia has always behaved like a lady to the manner born.'

Richenda frowned. She has never liked Hans to express

---

[4] She also tried to keep pigs, but the less said about that the better.

his admiration for me. Nor did it bode well that this sentiment could hardly have been addressed to Richenda. Despite all of Hans' efforts, she still refused to adopt the duties of the lady of the estate, leaving me to visit the sick, deal with the servants and attend to the one hundred and one little things that are always needed on an estate of this size. At least she drew the line at asking me to host the necessary dinner parties. Unfortunately, she did so by simply refusing to entertain. She complained she was far too busy, but in reality, the only duties she took with any seriousness were tending to her horse and mothering her children: Amy, adopted from amongst the survivors of the *Titanic*, and the twins she had given birth to recently – Alexander and Alicia. The latter were happy, contented, chubby little cherubs the like of which most new mothers dream. We had finally got a girl from the village to see to their needs, but only Richenda, Hans and I could control Amy, who was as daring and as bold as her flaming red hair.

'I suppose you think we should throw an engagement party?' said Richenda, challengingly.

'Oh no, I really don't think you should go to that sort of trouble,' I responded, throwing Bertram a helpless look. His lips twitched slightly.

'I believe Euphemia is of the opinion even that would be impolite before her mother's wedding. Such a thing should be hosted by her,' said Bertram.

'Then she must come here and host it,' said Richenda. A mulish look was developing on her face. I knew it well and knew that no good would come from it.

In fact, my mother had once visited the estate while staying with a local vicar - one I knew was a marriageable candidate who had been found unworthy. Unfortunately, rather than expose her daughter as a servant, she had hidden our relationship from Richenda. Worse still, Richenda, having learnt from my mother herself that she was the daughter of an Earl, had attempted to befriend her, and my mother had snubbed her. I believe this was as much from her dislike of Richenda, whose father she considered a jumped-up banker who was only made a baronet towards the end of his life, as it was for my sake. It seemed imperative to me therefore that they should not meet.

I looked over in appeal at Hans. He raised an eyebrow. 'Euphemia, this is your wedding and Bertram's, and nothing that you do not approve of will be undertaken.'

Bertram coughed, a sure sign of his embarrassment. 'Euphemia and I must discuss matters, but I believe she would be very happy to be married from your estate, Hans. It is a most generous gesture. Perhaps White Orchards will be finished in time for us to honeymoon there.'

I was caught mid-sip when he said this and the next few minutes entailed a lot of slapping me on the back and Richenda running around calling, uselessly, for smelling salts. When I had recovered, Bertram eyed me dolefully. He so wanted me to love his estate, rather than loving him despite it.

Hans, who had been involved in the back slapping, took my hand. 'I am sure we can do better than that,' he said. 'Not that your estate is not a lovely place by all accounts, Bertram. But a honeymoon should be in a place new to you both.' He winked at me. 'I will talk to him, sister.' For a moment I did not understand his last word, but then it dawned on me I would be Hans' sister-in-law. A strange thrill spread through my nerves. I was both elated to be related to such a gentleman and, I could not deny, slightly regretful Hans and I would never be any more than that. It seems scandalous to admit such, but there had been an undeniable attraction between us. However, Hans had needed to marry into money.

Hans looked deep into my eyes and I saw our thoughts were running along the same lines. 'Sister,' he said once more. He took my hand and briefly kissed it. Bertram coughed loudly.

I turned to him and placed my hand on his arm. 'When I think of how we all met,' I said, 'the final outcome is nothing short of a miracle. I am so lucky to have all of you in my life.' I gave him a sincere and heartfelt look. Hans might have been a brief romantic dream, but I had no doubt that Bertram, sodden estate and all, was the love of my life. It seemed that for once everything in my life was going well.

'I suppose it's just as well I bothered to get them an actual engagement present rather than merely offering our home,' said Richenda. All heads turned as one to look at her. Dear God, I prayed, don't let her have designed my wedding dress. Richenda has no more of a sense of fashion than her horse does.

'Really, my love?' said Hans. 'You have not mentioned this to me.' Even I could hear the warning in his tone.

Bertram spluttered about it not being necessary.

'What rot,' said Richenda, 'besides, it's something you will approve of, Hans. I have got us all tickets to the Anglo-German exhibition at the Crystal Palace. I have arranged the hotel and everything. We leave in three days and will be in London for four. I decided on the Carlton Hotel at Pall Mall. Their restaurant is run by Auguste Escoffier and offers the finest in *oaty cuisine*. And they have perfectly adequate provision for the children. You see, I have thought of everything.'

Bertram and I exchanged looks. I swear I saw his lips mouth, 'haute cuisine' while he rolled his eyes.

Towards the end of Richenda's pregnancy, in the late spring of 1913, Bertram and I had attended the Exposition Universelle et Internationale in Ghent. Richenda had been quite put out by being unable to attend.

'The twins are far too young to go to London,' said Hans.

'I will not go without them,' said Richenda, looking ever more like her horse when it is denied hay.

'Then it is settled,' said Hans. 'You will not go at all.'

At this point Bertram and I quietly left the table and backed out of the room. This was quite a sacrifice for Bertram as we had not yet had the pudding course. However, we had seen Richenda and Hans argue before. It was not unlike watching a storm, in this case Richenda, crash against a mountain, in that case Hans. Not something anyone would ever want to get caught up in.

Outside in the corridor Bertram said to me, 'What do you think will happen?'

'We'll end up going, but the twins will stay on the estate with their nursemaid.'

'And Hans?'

'I don't know,' I said. 'I don't think he will be at all happy about leaving the children here. Besides, you know how he reacts to Richenda trying to force him to do anything.'

'Hmm,' said Bertram. 'Badly.' He took my hand. 'We won't ever end up like that, will we?'

'I'm sure we'll argue,' I said. 'We are both people of passion. But once married we will have a new way of reconciling.'

Bertram frowned for a moment and then turned beetroot. 'Euphemia!'

'The vicarage where I grew up had a farm,' I said. 'I know more than most well-bred ladies.'

'I know,' said Bertram, 'but you should not admit it.'

'Even to you?'

'Especially not to me!' said Bertram. 'When there is nothing I can do about it.' He sighed. 'At least we will get to see Crystal Palace. I hear it is an outstanding spectacle. Besides, this is a small event by all accounts. We can't possibly have one of our adventures there.'

'Oh, Bertram,' I said. 'You had to say that.'

Chapter Two
Preparations For Our Non-Adventure

'I have no idea where she got those tickets,' said Hans for the hundredth time. 'I cannot find them in the household accounts and I am unaware of her having opened a bank account of her own.'

I looked helplessly at Bertram. Richenda had not taken me into her confidence about how her household matters were arranged. 'Kind of a matter between a man and his wife, don't you think?' said Bertram hopefully.

'At least she has given up on the ridiculous idea of taking the babies with her.'

'The babies?' said Bertram, growing a shade paler.

Hans sighed. 'I'm rather afraid Amy *is* going with you. Richenda has arranged for a London agency to send a nursery maid to the hotel.' He gave a wry smile. 'At least this time neither Richenda nor I have interviewed her, so we can hope nothing goes amiss.' Bertram harrumphed, and I looked at the floor. The capability of the Mullers to hire their own staff, particularly when it came to maids and chaperones, was becoming legendary in its disastrousness.

'At least you have it all sorted now,' said Bertram. 'It's not as though we will be away for long.'

Hans shrugged. 'Stay as long as you like. She's not talking to me anymore.'

Rather like a pair of pigeons sighting a man with a gun, Bertram and I made some distressed cooing sounds and backed away.

'This is a right old thing,' said Bertram when we were

alone in the library.

'I will be glad to see Crystal Palace,' I said. 'It is almost one million square feet! All plate glass and cast iron. It must be quite a spectacle in the sunlight.'

'Damned hot, I shouldn't wonder,' said Bertram. 'I had a gander at it myself one time I was in London, from across the park. Looked like a giant greenhouse. Why Albert wanted to put a whole load of stuff inside a big glass box I'll never know. Very showy. An Englishman would never have done it.'

'Hush,' I said. 'You know Hans' father was German.'

Bertram tugged at his collar. 'It would be good for everyone if that could be forgotten. Perhaps we could get him to change his name.'

I looked across at the folded copy of the *Times* that was lying on the reading desk. 'You think matters are as bad as that?'

'It's all very well saying that the Kaiser is related to King George the Fifth...'

'They are first cousins,' I said.

'Doesn't matter,' said Bertram. 'Richard has known the way the wind was blowing for some time now. He's been selling arms to the Germans and the French like billy-o. Trust a rat to smell a sinking ship.'

'Your brother would sell arms to the indigenous population of India if he thought he could get away with it. He is a warmonger, and worse yet, he is a profiteer on the back of it.'

'Hate to say it about my own flesh and blood, but of course he damn well is. He is also damned clever. It is very likely we are heading towards war.'

'You sound like Fitzroy.'

Bertram's eyes narrowed at the mention of the spy's

12

name. 'Have you seen him recently?'

I shook my head. 'No, thank goodness. That is the last thing I need.'

Bertram tilted his head on one side and regarded me with a look I knew only too well. 'What have I missed?' I asked with great misgiving.

'This exhibition is a last gasp at getting Germany and Great Britain to step back from the brink of war. I'd say he is bound to have a hand in it. For all we know he sent Richenda the tickets under some guise or other. He probably wants us there to do his dirty work.'

At this point I said a very unladylike word which I will not record here.

'Exactly,' said Bertram. 'I suggest you go and pry the truth out of Richenda, so we have some idea of what we're up against.'

'But the exhibition has been running since May,' I protested. 'Surely if anything were going to happen it would have happened by now.'

'On the contrary,' said Bertram. 'I would expect all cards to be out on the table only at the last gasp.'

I swore again.

'I think you need a brandy,' said Bertram. 'Your vocabulary appears to have developed an unfortunate bent.'

'Not before luncheon,' I replied. 'No, I shall go and beard Richenda in her den. If I stand between her and her meal I may stand a chance of getting the truth out of her.'

'I salute you,' said Bertram. He promptly sat down in a chair and pulled out his pipe. He stuck it between his teeth and opened the *Times*. He did not light his pipe, as Hans would have a fit if smoke got into his books, but this new affectation of his was not one I had taken to. At least now he had given up all pretensions of growing a beard, a practice that had left him itchy, bad-tempered, and somewhat resembling a sheep with mange.

I found Richenda in her boudoir arguing with her maid about packing. 'But I may stay longer,' she was saying. 'I cannot see how this affects you, Glanville. You always wear the same uniform.'

'I am referring to your personal wardrobe, ma'am,' said Glanville. 'Have you thought if you will go riding in London, or join one of your marches?'

'Ooh,' said Richenda. 'I had not given thought to that. Do you think Amy is too young to join us?'

'Yes, ma'am,' said Glanville to my great relief. Richenda occasionally listens to her new lady's maid. Glanville might be anywhere from forty to sixty years of age. Her face is a wrinkled walnut, with bright black currant-like eyes peeping out. Several pounds of hair are piled in plaits upon her head and she dresses in an appropriately plain style. Her thin lips rarely smile, but she has an acute sense of humour that Richenda only occasionally follows. She always speaks her mind, albeit respectfully, and she is a fully paid-up member of the suffragette movement. It is the latter that gained her the employment over other, younger maids. She is wiry and surprisingly strong for her small frame. The one time she discovered a gardener had left a ladder lying out, one that Amy had tripped over, causing many tears, but only a grazed knee, Glanville had turned tiger-like. Her admonishments had the young man shaking, even when he was given a calming beer in the kitchen, according to the butler, Stone, who spoke of Glanville in the most admiring of tones. Or as admiring as one might expect of such an extremely stoical man.

'Richenda, might I have a word?'

Richenda signalled to her maid to leave. Glanville backed out glowering. Richenda flounced out her skirts and sat down on an ornate chair. 'So, have you come as Hans' envoy?'

'No,' I said flatly.

'You know we are not speaking?'

'I have just heard,' I said. 'But you are husband and wife and it is not for me to interfere between you. Although I do think you might be more helpful to your maid. It is difficult to pack for someone when you don't know how long they might be from home. Even the number of stockings might cause a maid anxiety.'

'I suppose so,' said Richenda. 'But you never asked questions like that.'

'I could anticipate your needs better. Glanville has not been with us long.'

Richenda sighed. 'I will try to be better-tempered with her, but Hans has me on edge. All my nerves are vibrating.'

'Really?' I said. 'How unpleasant.'

'Apparently, it's good for you, if they are stimulated electrically, but not otherwise,' said Richenda. 'It was in this magazine I was reading. Quite fascinating. It can even help you reduce!'

Richenda has been on a lifelong quest to lose her excess weight, but this desire is rendered useless when placed alongside her love of cake.

'Actually, all I wanted to ask was how you came to purchase the tickets. I am quite unworldly when it comes to sending money through the post.' I was now lying through my teeth. I still sent money regularly to my mother, but Richenda was not to know this. 'It is the sort of thing I ought to find out about, if I am to run my own estate. I am sure there are many tips you could give me if you were so inclined.' I smiled, trying to think happy thoughts so the smile looked real – a trick Fitzroy had taught me.

'I'm not deceived,' said Richenda. 'You run much of this estate. That is fine by me. But if this is some backhanded way of Hans trying to get me to come up to scratch on my responsibilities when you leave, I will not have it. He can hire more servants. He has the money.'

At this point I came close to opening up about the troubles Hans might be about to face as a half-German national, but I held back. 'All right, you have seen through me,' I said. 'I want to know how you got the tickets. That is all. I am curious. Too curious for my own good.'

'Oh, very well,' said Richenda. 'Now it is all arranged, I don't see why I shouldn't tell. I got them from Richard. He's reaching out with an olive branch. I think his marriage has changed him. He wants to meet us all in London. He is especially keen to see the twins. You know his new wife still isn't pregnant. I think he is getting broody.'

Every alarm bell in my head began to ring at once, so that I missed her next few words. I only caught, 'As if I would do that, bah!'

'Of course,' I said as she seemed to be waiting for my reaction.

I was rewarded with a wide smile. 'Good. I knew you would see the sense of it. I am taking luncheon in my boudoir. Would you care to join me?' Much as I wanted to run to Bertram's side, I thought this prudent, and sat through a long and rather tiresome meal with her.

Richenda wanted to talk about nothing except the possibilities of my upcoming wedding, and whether or not I would wear a purple and green wedding dress to match my engagement ring.

It was not until early that evening that I managed to get Bertram alone. From the windows of my room I spotted him walking meditatively in the rose garden. Hans has some very pretty grounds and I too have spent time strolling and thinking deeply in them. I ran lightly down the stairs and out along the kitchen garden, which is only separated by a hedge from the roses.

'Bertram!' I exclaimed.

The poor man jumped a good four inches into the air. The pipe dropped from his lips and fell to the ground. 'Dash it all, Euphemia. You know I have a dicky heart. Are you trying to kill me?'

'Of course not, my darling,' I said, drawing close to him. 'But I very much fear someone else is.'

Chapter Three
Realising Richard's Relentlessness

'What the devil do you mean?' demanded Bertram.

I linked my arm through his. 'Let's walk a little way from the house,' I said. 'We don't want to get in the way of any of the gardeners working, do we?'

'Blast the gardeners,' began Bertram. Then he blinked. 'Oh, yes, of course. Wouldn't want to get in their way. How about the summer house over by the cricket ground?'

I reminded myself that a place is merely a place, no matter what previously occurred there. In this case, murder. As my father once said to me when I was young enough to quail at walking through the churchyard at night, 'There is not a place on God's green earth where man has not done damage to man. To walk among the restful dead is a blessing and a peaceful way.' I could only hope this particular deceased now rested peacefully, as we had solved their murder and their family were given justice.

Bertram, who had not really been involved in that case, wandered in and swept the wooden seat with his handkerchief for me. 'Lots of spiders,' he muttered.

We sat down. 'It transpires this whole trip Richenda is undertaking has been arranged by Richard. Your sister believes he is offering an olive branch as she and Hans have announced their intention of abandoning their claim to Stapleford House.'

I had not got even halfway through my speech before Bertram had leapt to his feet and was pacing. I continued in a calming tone though now his rapid movement was causing a crick in my neck.

'Dear God, does Hans know?'

'Of course not,' I said. 'He is too smart a man not to immediately see through such a ruse.'

'What do you think he is planning?' said Bertram. 'A runaway carriage? An accident with an automobile? A tram? Or a poisoning?'

'Do sit down,' I said. 'You're making me dizzy. I agree my own thoughts went exactly along those lines too. However, as we were walking across here, it occurred to me that we have spent a lot of time in Fitzroy's world of late. In normal life murder is not so commonplace.'

Bertram spoke through gritted teeth. 'We are both aware that my brother is not only capable of murder but has committed the crime at least once before.'

I did not disagree. 'And he is suspected. Even Richard must know he needs to tread lightly. Fitzroy and others are watching him.'

'But as long as he continues to lend money and manufacture arms they do not care,' said Bertram, and he struck the edge of the pretty pavilion fencing. It gave an ominous cracking sound.

'Killing Richenda and her children in one foul action would be too obvious. It could not be covered up.'

Bertram blanched at my putting the matter so baldly. 'When I think she wanted to take the twins. They are not even four months old!'

I curbed a smile. Bertram, unlike most men, likes children - even the very small and smelly ones. 'I agree that taking such small children to the metropolis is asking for all sorts of trouble, Richard aside. I am glad that Hans refused to let them go.'

'But you think the rest of us should go? Even Amy?'

'Amy is the one in least danger. She is not related by blood. I suspect in the case of Richenda, Richard is attempting to exert his influence over her again. They were close once. It might be to do with shares in the Stapleford Bank. I don't know about such matters.'

'Neither do I,' said Bertram. 'I made it clear to my father I would never take shares in his bank. It supported his arms business until that got going. It's all blood money. He took me at my word and left me none of it.'

'I know,' I said. 'And I am glad you took such a stance. I think in Richenda's case he wants to ensure that she and Hans do legally abdicate their interest in Stapleford House, and he may simply be keeping his options open when it comes to getting her on his side.'

'Would she fall for it?' asked Bertram.

'Who knows the strength of the bond of a twin?' I replied. 'I know Richenda now to be a good woman at heart, but I also know what she was like when she was under her twin's sway. If her marriage were stronger perhaps that would help, but…'

'How bad is it?' said Bertram. 'Has Hans got a mistress?'

'He would hardly tell me,' I objected.

'No, of course not,' said Bertram, blushing. 'I forgot who I was talking to for a minute.' Seeing my quizzical expression, he added, 'Damn it, Euphemia, you know you're an unusual woman. You're smarter than most of the chaps I have ever known. Even up at college.'

As Bertram's time at college was spent mostly drinking port, rowing for Oxford and gaining a very poor degree in PPE, I did not make the mistake of thinking this such a compliment.

'However, when it comes to us,' I said. 'I don't know if Richard knows we work for the government, but he may suspect. Certainly, we appear to tumble from one unseemly adventure into another with ever increasing frequency. An accident happening to us might not be so unbelievable.'

'Why us?' said Bertram, finally stopping pacing and facing me.

'Because we are engaged to be married, and despite it not yet being in the papers -'

'I must do something about that!' interjected Bertram.

'He may well expect that upon our marriage nature will take its course.'

Bertram stood there blinking at me for a while. Finally, he said, 'What, that you might have a child?'

'Goodness, Bertram, you make it sound as likely as me having an octopus!'

Bertram went beetroot. 'No. Well. I just assumed you wouldn't want to be a mother.'

'Of course I do,' I said. 'In time. Why, don't you want a chi -'

I did not get to finish my sentence as Bertram grabbed me into an embrace and locked his lips to mine. I found it not at all unpleasant. We stayed in the pavilion for some time.

A few days later I found myself sitting in Bertram's vehicle, with Rory McLeod in the back seat, as we motored up to London. After explaining the situation to Rory, I finished, 'We decided that if Richard intends something nefarious towards us we would rather he made his attempt away from the estate and the babies. Bertram and I - and you - have been in worse scrapes. We decided we can look after ourselves. But we both thought you should know what was going on.' I was sitting half turned towards him. It made for an uncomfortable position, especially given Bertram's glee at being out on the open road again. Only a gracious soul would describe his driving as erratic. Maniacal is the word I would be more apt to use.

Rory gave a deep sigh. His bright green eyes were almost hidden by the frown that drew his brows together. 'If I'd known I would not have encouraged you to go up to London,' he said. 'But of course, it's not my place to say so.' The last sentence was more growled than spoken. Rory was in a doubly difficult position with Bertram and I. Rory and I were once servants, with him my superior. We were once engaged. Subsequently, we have all three worked together as equals, and my engagement to Bertram must have created all sorts of feelings in the poor man. However, I knew better than to try and discuss them with him. Also, as Bertram's major-domo and occasional valet, Rory had given him his utter loyalty. How he felt about me I no longer knew. 'But I can see the sense of keeping it away from the babes,' he added. 'Do I take it we make a stand in London and deal with whatever he throws at us once and for all?'

'Would that we could,' said Bertram. 'The thought of knocking Richard over the head and burying him in a ditch is one of my fondest daydreams.'

'Aye,' said Rory, somehow making that single word sound very dark.

'But I am an English gentleman,' said Bertram. 'I will not stoop to my brother's methods.'

'I was afraid ye'd say that,' said Rory, who was becoming increasingly Scottish the unhappier he got.

'Maybe yon Fitzroy mannie will turn up and do the job for us.'

'No,' I said forcefully. 'The last thing we need is to get entangled with the Secret Service again.'

'But,' said Bertram, 'I think we should take the opportunity to make clear to Richard he is not to come near us or ours.'

'And how are you going to convince him of that?' asked Rory.

'We could offer to sign away our right to Stapleford Hall should we have children,' I said.

Rory definitely growled at this. 'Must that mannie get his way in everything?'

'It's a horrible place,' I said. 'Full of dreadful memories.'

'Actually,' said Bertram, 'I have some quite happy memories from when I was very little, and my godfather frequently came to stay. The servants were always very good to me. I often sneaked down to the kitchen for a small snack. They never gave me away.'

'You're hardly describing a family home,' I said.

'The only other home I have to offer you is fast sinking into the wetlands,' said Bertram. 'I thought you might like Stapleford Hall.'

'Rory won't let it sink,' I said confidently. 'And no, I don't want Stapleford Hall. Ever.'

'It is a Great House,' said Bertram, carefully sounding the initials as capitals. I almost laughed before I remembered he had no idea that Stapleford Hall would fit in my grandfather's stables with room to spare. I would have to tell him soon.

'No, thank you,' I said. 'You and the marshes are more than enough for me.'

Bertram signified his happiness by driving even faster. Rory and I hunkered down in our seats. And I, for one, prayed.

The Carlton Hotel at Pall Mall puts on a good show architecturally. Six storeys in height, along the roof line there is a selection of gables and turrets that I found not un-reminiscent of some of the eaves we had seen in Ghent, the whole thing topped off with a large dome. Periodically the façade is set with Doric or Ionic (I can never remember the difference) columns in fours. The edges of the building all end in a square pillar. The visible windows are large and many-paned, though I cannot speak to the lower servants' area. It is clearly a building created to be ostentatious - and thus it is perhaps not surprising that Escoffier had chosen it as the home for his London enterprise. To me it looked like a large and rather vulgar wedding cake.

Walking inside one immediately sees signs directing one to the Palm Court, which Bertram whispered in a loud aside was the very latest thing. I sometimes think he regrets buying an estate in the Fens for its distance from the metropolis as much as for its dampness. The man at the desk must have overheard him as he asked, in a most snooty manner, if we had reservations. Bertram was about to answer, but Rory moved past him and took the situation in hand. By the time we were escorted to the elevator, the motor had been stabled (or whatever one calls it), several bellboys were wheeling our luggage in large golden cages, and a veritable small army of attendants were escorting us across the lobby to the extremely large suite that had been hired for the Muller party. We were also given more information about the hotel than interested me by the clerk who accompanied us. As well as singing the praises of Escoffier, he told us the hotel had more than 250 bed and sitting rooms, many of which were en-suite, and all furnished in eighteenth-century English and French styles. Should one tire of London's attractions there were smoking rooms (men only), reading rooms, retiring rooms, hair-dressing rooms, a boy messenger service, a theatre box office, the Escoffier dining experience and more. Also, each room had a telephone line that could connect internally and externally. The last detail I paid the most attention to as it struck me that it could be of use should anything untoward occur.

We were on the fourth floor. As we exited the lift, I noticed that Bertram appeared to be fiddling in his trouser pockets. I did not feel I could comment on this with others around, but I attempted to nudge him significantly. He merely spared me a harried glance and went back to fiddling. As the bellboys deposited our luggage - obviously they had not ridden in the lift with us, but as if by magic had managed to arrive at the same time as us and our escort. The door was opened for us and the key handed to Bertram. The bellboys and their luggage cages started to stream inside. Had we really brought this much luggage? I stared at it a little bemused until I noticed the initials RM on one piece and realised Richenda's luggage had also arrived. The clerk followed my gaze.

'It came by train, madam,' he said. 'But we did not wish to put it into the suite until you arrived. Shall I send maids to unpack?'

'No, the other servants will be arriving shortly,' I said. The words came easily enough, but it felt strange to be on the other side of the master and servant divide. My engagement to Bertram had for ever removed me from my times below stairs. Fortunately, my mother had trained me all my life to become the mistress of a Great House. She had never given up hope of my grandfather forgiving her transgression in eloping with a curate. Speaking to the clerk, I could feel my early training returning to me. I suddenly understood that Bertram must not have supplied himself with enough coinage for tipping the staff. 'McLeod,' I said, 'if you could see the hotel staff are adequately enumerated for their service.' I then linked my arm through Bertram's and swept him inside.

Bertram almost at once sank into a chair and began mopping his head with his handkerchief. 'I had no idea they would send so many -' he began, but I put my fingers to my lips to shush him. While I waited for Rory to complete the transaction I looked around the reception area of our suite. The furniture was not to my taste, being mostly French, but it was freshly painted, and the cushions looked plump and comfortable. Several decanters had been set out to welcome us, ranging from sweet sherry through to ruby port. A plate of polished fruit sat on a central table, flanked by small plates covered in napkins and small silver fruit knives.

'If you could arrange for some tea, McLeod,' I said.

'Of course, madam,' answered Rory's voice with no tinge of the sarcasm he would have used had we been alone.

Doors seemed to lead off in all directions, but I decided to wait until all the hotel staff had left before I explored. Because of this I did not realise we were not alone until after Rory had shut the main door.

'How did you know I would be carrying change for the boys?' said Rory.

I smiled. 'You were close to being the perfect butler

when I first knew you,' I said. 'It did not occur to me you would be anything less than the perfect major-domo now.'

'It would have been dashed embarrassing if he hadn't had the money,' said Bertram.

'Aye, well. Better to embarrass me in front of the staff than you,' said Rory. 'As Euphemia well knows.'

'You were rather commanding,' said Bertram looking up from his chair in mild awe.

I shrugged. 'Remember how terrifying Mrs Wilson could be when she wanted. All housekeepers have that ability.' I was, of course, lying through my teeth. When I first knew Bertram, I would never have dreamed of lying, but now it was becoming all too common a circumstance. I needed to explain about my background, but I hadn't quite got around to finding the correct time to do so.

It was while I was wrestling with my moral fibre that a door opened and a nursery maid in uniform rushed into the room and embraced me.

'Euphemia,' cried Merry. 'It's been forever since I've seen you. Isn't this the greatest plan of Richenda's to get me to look after the children?'

Merry is my dearest friend. When I first joined Stapleford Hall as a clueless maid it was Merry who helped me adjust, covered for me and befriended me. Her name is really Mary, but she is of such a sunny disposition that she has earned herself the nickname of Merry.

'Step away, lass,' said Rory firmly. 'You can't behave like that with the master's future bride.'

Merry, who married Bertram's chauffeur, and now lives on his estate, looked from him to me in confusion. I held out my hand to display my ring. 'It's true. I am engaged to Bertram.' Merry paled. She took one step back and, to my horror, curtsied towards me. Before I could protest, the hotel door burst open once more. I had a brief glimpse of a harried-looking clerk as Richenda sailed past her. Following in her wake was Glanville and, before her, Glanville pushed a perambulator with Alexander and Alicia tucked up inside.

Chapter Four
Far Too Many Acquaintances and Family Members Join the Non-Adventure

Bertram jumped up. 'What the devil do you mean bringing the twins to London?' he cried.

Richenda didn't turn a hair but began to strip off her gloves. 'It is nice to see you too, Bertram. Did you have a good drive up? We came by steam train. Not that you bothered to enquire.'

'You took the twins on one of those infernal engines?' said Bertram.

'First class, of course,' said Richenda. 'It was rather nice. Better than being on the road with a whole load of lunatic drivers.' She looked pointedly at Bertram.

'Richenda,' I said quietly, 'does Hans know you have the children with you?'

'I am their mother,' said Richenda. 'Besides, there are more than adequate facilities here. I even arranged to have Merry with us.'

'Someone who your husband has forbidden to ever come near your children again after Amy escaped onto the roof while in her care,' said Bertram.

'Bah!' said Richenda. 'That could have happened to anyone. Amy has a spirited sense of adventure, it is hard to curb.

'Er, speaking of Amy,' I said, peering past them, 'where is she?'

'Why, she's…' said Richenda, turning around. 'Drat! She was right behind me. Did you see which way she went, Glanville?'

'So, she's in the hotel?' said Rory striding towards the door. 'I'll find her.'

Richenda made to follow. I caught her gently by the arm. 'He'll find her. I think you had better call your husband on the telephone and explain where the children are before he calls in the police. I don't suppose you left a note?'

'Why no,' said Richenda. 'Where else should the children be but with their mother.' A faint hint of pink on her cheeks was blooming into a fiery red.

'You should let him know they are safe,' said Bertram. 'The poor man is probably going out of his mind. I take it you sneaked out?'

'A certain amount of subterfuge was involved,' admitted Richenda.

Glanville looked increasingly uncomfortable. I also knew Richenda would quite rightly mind being berated before her own servants. Bertram's expression grew sterner by the moment. Any minute the whole situation would erupt into a full-blown family argument and from bitter experience I knew that would end extremely badly. 'Glanville,' I said. 'Would you mind taking the twins through to their nursery. Merry will show you the way. And perhaps then you could make a start on the unpacking? The hotel offered us their staff, but I felt certain you would want to see to your mistress' things yourself.'

Glanville's head snapped up. 'Indeed I would, ma'am,' she said.

'And Merry, the twins will need attending to after such a long journey. Please see if they are hungry and then put them down to sleep.'

Merry curtsied again. My eyes prickled, but I kept my composure.

The servants and the children exited the room. 'Now,' I said turning to Bertram and Richenda, 'the two of you can bicker as much as you like, but Hans needs to be informed of where his children are immediately.'

'I don't know how to use the machine,' said Richenda as sulkily as any child pulled up for its bad behaviour.

'Then I shall find my bedchamber and telephone him myself,' I said. Neither of them protested. 'You can come and find me when you have finished being difficult.' I began to sweep out of the room but stopped. 'Unless, of course, Rory returns without Amy, in which case you must fetch me at once.'

My bedchamber was luxurious, to say the least, and would hardly have looked out of place at Versailles. But in this particular moment I paid it scant attention. I picked up the telephone receiver, asked for a trunk call and then to be connected to the Muller estate. Stone answered the call and as soon as he heard my voice offered to fetch his master immediately. Hans came to the phone within moments. He was clearly out of breath.

'They're here,' I said. 'She brought them to London with her. I am so sorry, Hans. She came by train with Glanville. I had no idea she would do this.'

There was a long pause. Then Hans said in a cold voice, 'Do you suppose, Euphemia, that if I order my wife to return at once with the children she will do so?'

As Richenda had clearly not listened to Hans in the first place there was little I could say. The silence stretched between us. Eventually Hans said, 'I see.' Then he rang off. I had no sooner emerged from my bedchamber than Richenda shot out of another door rather like a cork out of bottle. 'Well?' she said. 'What did he say?'

'Nothing.'

'He must have said something! Did he ask to speak to me?'

'No.'

Richenda strode several paces towards me. Instinctively I backed away into the doorframe. She had the look of a woman who wanted to shake someone. A quick glance from side to side showed me that everyone else had beat a sensible, if not valiant, retreat. 'I told him the children were here,' I said. 'And that was all. Really.'

'Really?' Richenda continued to move slowly towards me, rather like an angry, fat cat that has finally managed to corner a mouse. I placed my hand on the doorknob behind me. I was fairly certain that I could step back and slam it in her face before she made contact.

'He did ask if I thought you would come home with the children if he ordered you to.'

Richenda froze. Her voice rose more octaves than seemed natural. 'Ordered me? Ordered me! What did you say?'

'What could I say to such a ridiculous question?' I responded, attempting to hedge my bets in a way Richenda would not spot. Either she would become the doting wife and say obviously, yes, she would go home, or she would start spouting - well, raving - about men asserting their authority over women. I thought the latter most likely. 'I said nothing,' I said.

'Thank you,' said Richenda. 'I knew I could count on you. If you will excuse me.' She turned away and strode into her room. Then came the sound of a door slamming and what I assumed Richenda felt were discreet sobs.

Bertram popped his head out of a door. 'Is someone

drowning a cat?' he asked.

They say time heals all wounds. Certainly, this seemed to be the case from the glee on Richenda's face as we hailed a cab to take us to Crystal Palace. She clearly didn't have a care in the world. I, on the other hand, was extremely tired from a disturbed night waking at every slight noise that I feared heralded Hans' angry arrival. But he did not come.

Amy had been found in the kitchens, chatting to the pastry cook, a ferocious individual who apparently scared all the staff, but who had been feeding Amy titbits and commenting on the level of vanilla needed in the crème pâtissière. Apparently, the staff had assumed she was the child of a fellow staff member who was waiting for her parent to come off duty. Amy, of course, did nothing to disabuse them of this idea. So, Rory had quite a lot of trouble finding her as the staff clubbed together to shield her from what they felt was either management or guests' prying eyes. Eventually he delivered her to Bertram - Richenda still being indisposed.

'But dammit,' said Bertram to me over breakfast that morning, 'if the imp didn't have me fixing a broken doll within minutes of my attempting to scold her.'

'Did you fix the doll?' I asked. Bertram is not, to my knowledge, mechanically inclined and most dolls, especially the expensive ones Richenda buys Amy, are strung together in a positive lattice of inner framework.

'No,' said Bertram. 'I only managed to pop its head off. I was terrified she was going to start blubbing like her mother, but instead she laughed like a duck stuck down a drain. An extraordinary sound.'

'I take it Rory fixed it?'

'Oh yes. Gets that kind of skill from his father I expect.'

I paused, a spoon of marmalade poised over a rather thin-looking piece of toast that I was concerned might not bear the conserve's weight. 'His father?'

Bertram nodded and spoke through his eggs, most unattractively. 'You know, grocer and all that. Weights and measures.'

'But…' I began, and then dropped the subject. 'Is Amy to accompany us to the Palace?'

Bertram nodded. 'Her mother says it will be educational.'

'It will be downright calamitous,' I said forebodingly.

'I count us lucky Merry talked her out of bringing the babies.'

'She couldn't have thought that was a good idea,' I said.

'This is Richenda,' said Bertram. 'An angry Richenda.'

'You're right,' I said and swept the toast into my mouth before it broke under the weight of its orangey load. 'We should count ourselves lucky.'

'You know, my love,' said Bertram. 'I think perhaps we should work on your table manners.' It took all my will power not to post my poached egg down the front of his shirt.

Now, as Bertram, Richenda, Rory, Amy and I waited for the cab, I too began to feel some of the excitement. The event Bertram and I had witnessed in Ghent was amazing and this smaller exhibition could not compare on that front. But I was looking forward to seeing such a giant glass structure. Originally built on Prince Albert's instructions for his Great Exhibition, it had fallen on hard times and almost been pulled down, when the nation stepped in and bought it. The thought of seeing such a giant jewel of a place thrilled me. Although I expected it to be very hot inside and had accordingly worn my lightest dress.

'Do you know it is three times larger than St Paul's,' I said to Bertram as we all piled into the cab. 'It is 128 feet in height and the light is of such quality that trees flourish inside the structure.'

'Hmm,' said Bertram. 'I'm afraid Richenda wants me to look after Amy. Have you frisked her for catapults?'

'I wonder who cleans all the glass,' said Rory. 'That must be a terrible task.'

'It was entirely dismantled from Hyde Park and rebuilt on Penge Common,' I said. 'Without any of it breaking. What a feat.'

'What?' said Richenda. 'I thought it was still in Hyde Park.'

I shook my head. 'I read up on it this morning. There was a most informative pamphlet in the lobby and the concierge was also most helpful. Apparently, not long after the Great Exhibition finished, the whole Palace was removed to South London. It is now on the top of Penge Peak next to Sydenham Hill. An area described as an affluent suburb of large villas.'

Richenda regarded me with horrified fascination. 'This is not what I was expecting at all,' she said. Then she turned to Bertram. 'I hope you have enough money to pay the cabbie, Bertram.'

Bertram shot a look at Rory, who sighed deeply and nodded.

Amy had her nose pressed against the window, staring out at the mysteries of London. The street traffic remained a mixture of horse-drawn carriages and motor vehicles.

Drivers of each mode of transport seemed to feel theirs should take priority on the road. This occasioned enough near-misses that I kept my eyes facing forward. I had driven with Bertram often enough to have a certain sangfroid when it came to near collisions and I assumed that London cabbies were more apt at avoiding them than my beloved.

'Why didn't we go in Uncle Bertram's automobile?' asked Amy.

'We wouldn't have fitted,' said Richenda.

Amy pouted. 'It is so slow being drawn by horses.' She sniffed. 'And why is there a servant in the cab with us, Mother? You said we should travel separately. Isn't that why you made Glanville travel third class on the steam express?'

Amy has already lost the Irish lilt she had in her voice and appears to have no memory of her previous family. All of these were Irish immigrants travelling steerage on the *Titanic* when it sank. It is miraculous that she escaped as most of the people on the lower decks did not. There are many stories that come from that night that show both the best and worst of humanity. Richenda and I, who were both on the *Carpathia*, which steamed to her rescue, have chosen not to speak to her about the tragedy until she comes to us with questions. Her near-death experience and loss of family is perhaps why we allow her so much latitude, but I could not help bridling at her comment. Before I could speak though, Bertram cut in.

'Rory McLeod is my major-domo and my friend,' he said. 'Major-domo is like an estate manager, only more than that. You need to learn, Amy, that those fortunate enough to employ others have a duty to respect them as fellow human beings.'

'Are you saying that because you are marrying Aunt Euphemia and she used to be a maid?' said Amy.

Richenda reached over and boxed Amy on the ears. 'Enough. You know better than this. I will send you back to the hotel if you do not behave yourself. If you move more than two feet from my side I will send you back to your father who will thrash you for your disobedience.'

Amy shed a few tears over her sore ears, but she clearly did not believe the threat any more than the rest of us. We knew Hans would never raise a finger against his daughter.

'And,' said Richenda, obviously realising she was losing control, 'you will have no pudding for a fortnight.'

Amy paled at this and promised vehemently to be good. Although not biologically related to Richenda, she has acquired her fondness for cake. However, being a very active child, this has not yet shown in her form.

Throughout the whole conversation Rory stared ahead.

'Did you really send Glanville third class?' asked Bertram. 'I'm not sure I would have dared.'

'I asked her where she would be comfortable,' said Richenda. 'She said third. She is most traditional. She keeps misplacing my more modern clothes but is an expert at keeping things tidy and Amy heeds her more than me.' She added the last in a low voice that only Bertram and I heard.

'Look! Look!' cried Amy.

Ahead of us on a hill stood a shining edifice. The autumn sun had come out from behind the clouds and Crystal Palace looked for all the world like something out of a fairy tale. I found myself holding my breath as we wound up the road towards it. Two stories high, the centre of the roof rose into a barrel vault. The true marvel was the amount of glass visible. Only the thinnest of cast ironwork seemed to hold the panes in place. It was all glass.

'What's that canvas thingy?' asked Bertram, pointed to part of the roof. 'Is it broken?'

'It is one of the methods of keeping the temperature inside at an ambient level,' said Rory. 'They are shade cloths which also soften the interior lighting. There is also a remarkable ventilation system -'

Richenda cut him off. 'Lovely,' she said as the carriage drew up. 'Bertram, pay the man and let us go in!'

I would have liked my first experience of Crystal Palace to have been a full appreciation of its beauty. I had hoped to stand next to one of the many trees inside and simply gaze up and around. In truth, the Anglo-German Exhibition had little interest for me. However, I had barely walked through the doors when I heard a voice that jumped out at me. I remembered it from our days at Stapleford Hall.

'I tell you I am not one to manipulate the cards,' said the staunch voice of Madame Arcana, self-styled medium and covert British Intelligence agent. 'They say what they say.'

Bertram had stiffened at my side. He pivoted on his heel rather like a gun dog pointing at the fallen bird. 'Is that…?' he said.

Amy was already tugging Richenda forward. 'Meet at the tea shop in an hour?' she called. I nodded. 'You'd better go with 'em, McLeod,' said Bertram. 'She'll never control Amy on her own.' Rory nodded and headed off.

'He never met her, did he?' said Bertram. 'I know he's signed the same stuff as us, but introducing agents and all that, I don't know the protocol.'

'We're not agents,' I said. 'We help out sometimes.'

'I suppose so,' said Bertram. 'If we were agents they would likely pay us. Not that a gentleman should care about such things if he's serving his country.'

'Fitzroy certainly appeared to be well-paid,' I said. 'Oh look, she's seen us. She's waving us over. We either make a run for it now or go over.'

'She doubtless knows what we're going to do,' said Bertram. 'And there'd be no point in her waving to us if we were going to run off. So, we must head over. If you believe in all that stuff.'

'I don't,' I said. 'But I do believe in being polite.'

'We should have moved on when we had the chance,' muttered Bertram. He took my arm and linked it through his. 'If she says anything about how she foresaw the two of us becoming betrothed I will not be responsible for my actions.'

Our beckoner was standing in front of a booth, the curtains of which were closed. Above it ran the legend, 'The Greatest Medium the World has Ever Seen'. The drapes were purple with golden tassels and had mystical symbols running down both sides in shades of red and gold. Presumably one entered into the depths for a reading. For now though, she stood outside, hands on her hips, looking more like an outraged dowager than a master of the arcane arts.

Madame Arcana, who would never see her fortieth year again, but who was otherwise ageless, was dressed much as she always was. She wore a floral-patterned dress that clung to the sides of her ample hourglass figure. This time it was turquoise with extravagantly large lilies. Around her neck were multiple loops of pearls, some of which hung down past her waist, and on her head was a purple turban, decorated with a short peacock feather. She was unmissable. The man she had been addressing stood with his back to us. From the hunch of his shoulders we gathered he did not like the public display of their conversation.

As we reached them, Madame Arcana said, 'There you are, Eric. This was why we couldn't go inside before. I told you they were coming.'

Fitzroy glanced at us and glowered. 'Fine,' he said. 'Let's get inside before the whole of London sees us.'

Bertram gaped, and I felt something inside me sag with resignation. Fitzroy, who is deliberately one of the least remarkable featured people one could ever meet, held up the side of the curtain for us to enter. Today his hair was as dark as his eyes. He wore a good but plain long coat and held an innocuous-looking brown walking cane. I imagined it could be made to explode or bristle with blades or some such thing.

'It is made of wood,' said Madame Arcana.

'What is?' said Bertram.

'His cane. He hurt his foot when he -'

'Enough,' growled Fitzroy. 'What the devil are you two doing here? And why did you tell her you were coming and not me?'

The inside of the tent was suitably dim. A total contrast to the brilliance of the Palace outside, it took my eyes as much time as it was taking my mind to adjust to the situation. Fitzroy jerked out a chair in front of me and helped me into it. Bertram blundered around to my left until he too was seated. Fitzroy pulled out a chair, turned it the wrong way around and sat down legs apart. I could not see clearly yet, but the unusualness of the position left me feeling awkward in a hot sort of way.

As I adjusted to the darkness, I realised it wasn't pitch

black. There were two lanterns hung in the corner. Madame Arcana turned them both up and I saw that we were seated about an oaken, round, occasional table. While our seats were normal chairs, the one the medium took for herself had a high rectangular back that rose above her head and had sturdy armrests. It was reminiscent of a throne. This was no doubt why Fitzroy had chosen such an ungentlemanly position. He is never one to be outdone by one of his own people.

'We did not tell Madame Arcana we were attending,' I said. 'We knew nothing about it until very recently. Richenda Muller gave us the tickets as an engagement present.'

Madame Arcana reached over and touched Bertram lightly on the arm. 'I won't say it, dear, if it will upset you. But I did see it.'

Bertram frowned. I interrupted before he could work out what she was saying.

'I suppose I should not be surprised you are here, Fitzroy, or is it Lord Milton today?'

'Eric will do in here.'

'He's a little tense,' said Madame Arcana. 'There is no way to win the game he has been asked to play.'

'A card game?' said Bertram.

Madame Arcana chuckled. 'Ah, that's only a small part of it. Eric wants me to do readings for the German contingent and convince them to increase their diplomatic efforts. But of course, I cannot force any card onto the table. I suppose I could choose to misread them, but it only takes someone with a very little knowledge to tell when someone is saying the opposite of what is being shown. I do have my reputation to consider.'

'I am asking you to do this for the sake of your country,

woman,' said Fitzroy.

'I am not a card sharp,' said Madame Arcana. 'I cannot make certain cards appear.'

'Actually, it is a damn difficult thing to do,' said Bertram. 'I spent a good part of my teens trying to learn how to do it. Never could.' He glanced at me. 'One of my disreputable cousins kept cheating me out of my tuck money and I needed to know how he was doing it.'

'Fascinating,' said Fitzroy, not meaning it in the least. 'But the whole point of having you here, Arcana, was to help the peace process.'

'Does it have to be cards Madame Arcana reads?' I asked.

'It is what I am known for.'

'But you do excellent séances,' I said.

'Bless you, dear.'

Fitzroy's frown lightened. 'Actually, that gives me an idea. If I slipped one of the German delegates into a séance and you happened to say…'

'I suppose that could work.' She turned to me. 'I said I wouldn't do a séance for the contingency as a whole as they were carrying a great deal of negative energy around with them. But if we had you and your husband-to-be there, and maybe another of your party, we could weaken their negativity.'

'Whatever it takes,' said Fitzroy.

Bertram coughed. 'I don't wish to be rude, but it sounds rather as though you are pinning the hopes of the nation on a magician's trick. No offence, Madame.'

Madame Arcana bowed slightly. 'I am the real article, Mr Stapleford, but I do, on occasion, shall we say *tune my gifts* for the sake of my country.'

'Bah!' said Fitzroy.

'Is it that desperate?' said Bertram.

Fitzroy took a handkerchief from his pocket and wiped his forehead. 'It is part of a cascade I am running.' Bertram frowned. Fitzroy sighed loudly. 'You set a series of incidents in motion that appear unrelated, but all reinforce a central idea. In this case that it serves neither the interests of Germany or England to go to war. Madame Arcana is but one small step in the process, but she is proving disproportionally difficult.'

'The target of this cascade being the German contingent over here for the exhibition,' I said. 'Are they important enough to make a difference to the political situation back in Germany?'

'They are all I have to work with,' said Fitzroy.

'Is the situation really that dire?' said Bertram, still seeking a clear answer to his questions. 'Do you expect war to break out any day?'

'No,' said Fitzroy. 'It may be months, even a year or two, before we hit the brink, but right now the course is set.'

I leant back in my seat. In my mind's eye I saw a dream I had while staying at the Stapleford's Hunting Lodge many years ago. At first, I thought I was dreaming of men marching to war, but then in the dream I realised the men were already dead and were marching to the afterlife. There had been row upon row of them, reaching numbers my mind could not comprehend. Rory had been among them.

'Breathe, dear,' said Madame Arcana. 'Nothing is ever set in stone. We only ever glimpse possibilities.'

'What happens when you read your tarot cards?' I demanded.

Madame Arcana's shoulders slumped. 'When I ask

about the possibility of peace between the two nations they always come up with war. I fear if I read for the German gentlemen, in that as they are all nobles or diplomats, war will be the strongest feature of the reading. I have tried over and over, but the cards are clear.'

'But you said nothing is set in stone,' I said.

'Some possibilities are more likely than others,' said the medium sadly.

'A clerk in the home office would tell you the same,' said Fitzroy. 'Anyone who reads the papers knows which way the wind is blowing. My job is to see if we can change the course of things.'

'And if that isn't possible?' said Bertram.

'In that case I am tasked with learning as much about the German armed forces and tactical plans as possible from the delegation.'

'I see,' said Bertram. 'This would be the game you cannot win.'

Chapter Five
Messages From The Other Side

'I do hope you're not referring to war,' said Fitzroy severely. 'Because I can assure you that His Majesty's Armed Forces are the best in the world and can trounce any enemy.'

'But at what cost,' I said quietly.

'Any man would be honoured to give his life for his country,' said Fitzroy.

'Of course,' said Bertram stoutly.

'What about the mothers, daughters and wives who would lose their menfolk?' I said, but only Madame Arcana paid me any heed.

'Mankind learns slowly,' she said. 'And women generally pay the price.' Bertram and Fitzroy both opened their mouths to speak, but she continued. 'I take it you are agreeing with me, Eric, that war is coming whatever you do today?'

Fitzroy closed his mouth and furrowed his brow. It was some time before he spoke, but all of us waited on his words. I half expected some quip from him about Madame Arcana knowing more clearly with her abilities, but when he finally spoke, his voice was grim. 'I do not relish the thought of war. I will do everything I can, to my fullest ability, to avert it, but I do not see how to avoid it.'

'But your cascade,' I said

He pressed his lips together in a thin smile. 'I empty out my entire box of tricks, Euphemia, and yet it does not appear to be enough to change the collision course that both sides seem determined upon. If you mingle among the general public at this exhibition - one designed to strengthen ties between England and Germany - you will witness everyday men and women openly discussing their dislike of the Germans. The hostility is already entrenched, and it will take a more powerful man than I to lift it.'

'But you will still try?' I said.

'Of course,' said Fitzroy. 'It is my job to protect our realm in whatever function I can serve. At this time, I believe it would serve us best to avoid war, but I will not make the decision. However, since you are so keen to be a dove at this time, Euphemia, I take it I can count on you and Bertram to aid me in the following days.'

'Of course,' said Bertram at once. 'Whatever you need.'

'Bertram,' I said urgently. 'Have you forgotten our situation?'

'What situation?' said Fitzroy.

'Nothing,' said Bertram. 'We're dealing with it.'

'Euphemia?' said Fitzroy.

'It is merely my brother up to his old tricks,' said Bertram. 'Family business.'

'So, this is how you will be in marriage?' said Fitzroy to me. 'An obedient wife whose husband speaks for her.'

I knew he was attempting to needle me. I placed my hand on Bertram's arm. 'My fiancé appears to want to keep the situation between us, so I will only confirm that Richard Stapleford is indeed making a nuisance of himself once more and possibly, this time, to deadly effect.'

'Hmm,' said Fitzroy. 'I cannot have your focus divided. It is too important. Obviously try and not let yourselves get murdered, but otherwise, forget Stapleford. I need your help.'

I felt this was a bit rich considering he hadn't even known we were going to be there that day but said nothing. He caught my eye. 'Madame Arcana was sure you would be here today.'

'The British Secret Service is relying on omens and portents now, is it?' said Bertram. 'How long before you are giving us magic potions to drink?'

'I think Eric only wants the séance today,' said Madame Arcana. 'You'll need to increase my fee if you want more.'

Fitzroy threw her a black look. She winked back at him. Fitzroy's scowl deepened yet further. I stifled a giggle and unfortunately drew attention to myself. 'Ah, yes, I think the séance would seem more believable if there were some normal people there. Euphemia, why don't you attend with Richenda? I believe modern women are into these kinds of things.'

'I'm not sure,' said Madame Arcana. 'Euphemia is unusually strong with death.'

Fitzroy stood up. 'None of your nonsense for me, please, Annie. I'm not one of your stooges.' He looked at me. 'It'll be in an hour. Be here. Bertram, with me.'

Bertram threw me an apologetic look. 'I'll see you afterwards,' he said and followed Fitzroy out of the booth.

'Do not take it to heart, Euphemia,' said Madame Arcana. 'Eric is always at his sternest when he feels a situation slipping from his control. He would call it his professional demeanour. I would term it deeply concerned. I do feel for him. Whatever he does today will not please his masters.' Her voice did not change but her eyes seemed to lose focus on me. Instead her gaze seemed to fall on a place far away. 'There are very dark times ahead. However, if it helps I can see that Bertram will not be called upon to serve. His heart is too weak, and Eric has a way of surviving, so do not fear for either of them.'

I pushed to the back of my mind the memories of my dream, but Madame Arcana read, at least, my continuing concern. 'If you are thinking about the butler, McLeod, his fate is uncertain, but as your path joins with Mr Bertram, then so will your paths part and yet still cross.' She gave herself a little shake and her eyes returned to normal. 'Whatever happens, your little brother is far too young to ever be caught up in it all. Who knows but it may bring him good fortune in a backhanded way?'

'You know about Joe?'

'Eric gave me quite a full briefing about you, when he first acquired you as an asset. He checks these things out very thoroughly. Laboriously goes through the paperwork to gain his information. No matter how enigmatic he tries to appear, a lot of what he learns is through very ordinary leg work. I, however, get a lot of information from the other side.'

'Ah,' I said.

Madame Arcana lent forward and tapped my hand lightly. 'I mean the Germans, dear. What else could I have meant?' She winked at me. Then she stood and showed me out of the booth. 'Well, Miss St John, a most interesting reading, I am sure you will agree. I would be delighted if you chose to return for the séance later.' Then she stepped back and disappeared behind the drapes. I was left standing alone in Crystal Palace. The autumn sun remained high and bright, but for me the day was now quite overcast.

I found Richenda seated in a tea shop, sharing a plate of cakes and a cup of tea with Amy. She waved at my approach. 'Do sit down. I'll say this for the Germans, their pastries are wonderful and so filling. This chocolate torte looks so slim, but it has the weight of a thousand bricks – a thousand divine-tasting bricks, but I am sure I will not be able to move for hours.' At this point she paused to insert a large section of a cream bun into her mouth. An expression of bliss crossed her face. Amy grinned at me.

'So far we have not seen very much of the exhibition, Aunt Euphemia,' she said. 'Despite the clever shades, Mama was finding it rather hot, so I suggested we should have a pot of tea.'

'And of course, where there is tea there must be cake,' I said.

'Of course, Aunt,' said Amy with a perfectly straight face.

'Pour your aunt a cup of tea,' said Richenda. 'Where's Bertram?'

'He met someone he knew,' I said, accepting the tea and earning the favour of Amy but refusing the offer of the final fancy cake.

'Men!'

'Rory?'

'Oh, McLeod wandered off to look at something German and mechanical. He could hardly act as my escort, could he?'

'Hmm,' I said, considering. 'As a married lady you have a latitude that I do not. I had hoped he had stayed around. I have been invited to a séance and I hoped you might join me. It is not really for Amy.'

Richenda's eyes lit up. 'How exciting.'

'You may remember her. She once came to Stapleford Hall. A Madame Arcana?'

'I was never entirely sure about her,' said Richenda. 'But I recall that she did favour you. Something about how death hung about you.'

'Yes, well, I'd really rather it didn't,' I said quickly. Amy's eyes had gone very wide.

'I'm sure they have page boys,' said Richenda. 'I'll page McLeod. He can take care of Amy. After all, he works for the family.'

As Bertram remained missing I silently sacrificed Rory, who I knew had no love of child minding. He was promptly found and told of his duties. He took one look at my face and didn't protest. Richenda gathered her various possessions - her umbrella, her bag, her scarves, her hair pins and hat pins that she always had inadvertently scattered about her person, her handkerchiefs that dislodged themselves from her sleeves and, of course, the testament to her enjoyment of the tea shop: a small molehill of crumbs.

'I'm sure she never used to take so much around with her,' I said in an aside to Rory. 'Even her personal bag appears heavy, as if she has filled it with ashtrays and perfume bottles.'

'Maybe she has,' said Rory. 'Woman seems odder to me than she ever was at Stapleford Hall. By the way, I thought I saw your Bertram off with yon mannie whose name we do not mention.'

'Indeed. Is that why you accepted your charge without complaint?'

'If the worst I have to do for King and Country on this day is mind a precocious wee brat, it'll be a damn sight easier than what I've been called on to do before.'

There was no way I could defend Fitzroy, so I simply nodded. Rory and I sighed in unison.

'Do come in, ladies and gentlemen,' said Madame

Arcana holding back the drape herself. 'I have managed to divert the flow of visitors away from my little tent, so we can be assured of absolute privacy. This will not only please the spirits but allow you to ask whatever questions you wish.' She gave a little smile. 'Of course, I have chosen a select grouping, but if you remain shy about voicing your enquiries, be assured: when in a trance, I can understand and convey meaning from the merest hint. However, I cannot vouch for the spirits. The terser your question, the more likely they are to respond in kind.' She chuckled at this point. 'They do like our attentions, the spirits. I find those that respond most quickly to the call of the medium are often the ones most bored on the other side.'

We stood in an uncomfortable group outside the entrance that Madame Arcana held open. None of us, it appeared, wished to go first. 'Excuse me for asking,' said a gentleman to my left, in a slight German accent, 'is she suggesting that Gott's heaven is not a paradise?' I looked round to see a dapper gentleman in his middle years regarding me with earnest brown eyes. My face must have registered surprise.

'I am sorry if I have offended,' said the gentleman. 'I believe it is not the custom here, nor is it at home, to address a lady without introduction, but am I a religious man. I have only accepted this invitation to attend out of diplomacy. But if the - how do you say, inter-between person - is going to cast aspersions on Gott's good graces I cannot enter.'

'My dear sir,' said Richenda, turning to speak before I could answer. 'Have you heard of the Church of England? We founded Christianity. This is the most Christian country, and Madame Arcana is a good Christian woman.'

The gentleman frowned at her confusing response, but before he could speak I said, 'May I present to you Mrs Hans Muller, the sister of Richard Stapleford, of whom you may have heard.'

'Indeed yes,' said the gentleman, the frown remaining on his face. 'He is most often visiting the fatherland and is well known among the upper levels.'

I pursed my lips to prevent a smile. The German man's accent was indeed slight, but his vocabulary needed some work. 'May I introduce myself,' I said, 'without seeming forward, I hope? I am Euphemia St John and my widowed mother is shortly to marry a bishop. I cannot say she would approve of this entertainment, but neither would she cast me from her door. My own father was a vicar and he encouraged me to have an open mind as long as I held God's tenets in my heart.'

'He sounds like a very wise man,' said the German. 'I am sorry for your loss. I am Klaus Von Ritter. I am part of the delegation from Germany visiting our joint exhibition.'

'I confess I have not yet had time to see much of exhibition,' I said. 'But I am looking forward to it. It is in such a wonderful setting and I have already had the opportunity to try a wonderful sweet called, I believe, a torte?'

'Was it chocolate?' said Klaus. 'It is my own dear wife's favourite.'

'Yes, and quite delicious,' I said, stepping back on Richenda's foot before she could protest I had not tried the tart for myself.

'May I enquire if you hope to hear from your deceased father?'

'Not at all,' I said. 'My father was a most diligent man of the cloth and worked hard for all his parishioners. He rarely referred to his own demise except to say he felt he hoped to finally find some peace there!'

At this the German laughed out loud. 'I am sure your father and I would have got along famously. These diplomatic tours are endless. Do not mistake me, I have all the time in the world for actual diplomacy, but these shows, exhibitions, dinners, etc., go on and on.'

'I am sorry you are not enjoying our hospitality more,' said Richenda snappily.

Klaus flushed scarlet. 'Ah, mein Gott, meine Frau. Es tut mir leid…'

'What on earth is the man babbling about?' said Richenda. 'Has he gone mad? Do I need to call someone?'

'I believe he has merely reverted to his native language,' I said. 'The heart of the matter is that he meant no offence.'

'Humph,' said Richenda. 'If no one else is going first, then I will lead the way.' She strode off.

'Sprechen sie Deutsch, Fraulein?'

'I am afraid not, sir, but your intent was clear. As one who has sat through sermons many times, I fully understand that even the best of events can become tedious.'

'Thank you,' said Klaus. 'Can I say it is a pleasure to meet a tolerant and intelligent young English woman.' He paused. 'You may not have heard but there were protests outside our hotel. I do not understand why some of your countrymen are so opposed to our presence.'

'My father would have said we are all children of God,' I said.

Klaus smiled. 'Indeed. Let us hope that those that make the big decisions do not forget that.' He offered me his arm. I knew this my mother would disapprove of even more than my attending a séance, but for the sake of King and Country I took it. Besides, he appeared a very nice gentleman, whom I found fatherly in his manner. Our arms had barely linked before there was a flash of a camera. Klaus swore in German. I did not try and translate. A man, who had been lingering behind Klaus, and who I realised must have been some kind of aide, responded in the same language and urged Klaus forward. We entered the tent. I found myself seated between Klaus and a woman who smelled of fish. The odour was strong enough to make me want to reach for my handkerchief. I stole an askance glance at her, but she appeared to be dressed as a fashionable matron of status. The aide sat on the other side of her and kept up a diplomatic façade. Other than Madame Arcana, there was a young couple, who sat very close together, to the extent I felt certain he must be holding her hand under the table. Both of them appeared very nervous. And finally, there was a man so unremarkable that I assumed he must be one of Fitzroy's men.

Madame Arcana fussed with the lamps, dimming the lights and squeezing her amble frame around the table with many apologies. 'I prefer not to have help with the preparations,' she exclaimed, 'the aura of others can pollute the setting. Now, if we are ready, please place your hands upon the table so your little finger is touching the little finger of the person next to you. A light touch if you please, and your own thumbs should be touching. Thus.' She demonstrated. 'This is the circle of invocation which I shall shortly activate. Should it be broken by any person here the spirits will flee, and I will possibly be endangered. Therefore, can I ascertain that all present are willing.' She cocked her head to one side in the shadows and I imagined her smiling. 'I do not ask you to be believers. Your belief or disbelief has no effect on my talent, but I do ask that you comply with my instructions. If you are not willing, or able, to do so, may I ask you leave the tent now. I only want those to remain who, on their honour, will obey the rules of the séance.'

I thought it all a bit heavy-handed. Madame Arcana had been much more informal in our previous encounters. I assumed she was putting on a show for Klaus. I became quite enthralled as to what she might do for the sake of Fitzroy's cascade.

'Silence then please,' she said. Then she gave the familiar medium's call. 'Is there anybody there who wants to speak to anybody here?'

Silence reigned. Madame Arcana waited some moments, heightening the suspense. Then she repeated, 'Is there anybody there who wants to speak to anybody here?' Then she gave a low moan. Her voice, when it next spoke was lower in tone, 'What the bleedin' heck are you two up to? Dominic, you take that girl back home now. Shame on you.'

'Uncle 'Arry?' exclaimed the male half of the young couple. 'We ain't done anyfin' wrong. You know that. But Edith's mother, she don't like me.'

'Then you convince her otherwise, lad. Your mam raised you better than this. Poor wee thing is terrified. This ain't no way to start a life together.'

'But we'll be in such trouble if we go back,' said the young woman. Her voice cracked with tears.

'It'll be worse if you don't, young lady. Take it from one that knows.'

I heard Richenda give a little gasp of amazement.

Madame Arcana's voice changed yet again. 'Hallo, my

57

darling,' she said in what came close to a well refined male voice, 'How's the little 'un?'

The woman who smelled of fish cried out, 'Oh, Edward, it that you?'

'Yes, my love, it's me.'

'Maurice is doing very well at the prep school. Of course, he cried when we heard you were not found among the survivors, but he is young enough that...' She broke down in tears. 'Oh, Edward, tell me you didn't suffer? Tell me you weren't trapped below decks.'

'No, my love. I was helping the ladies into the life boats. Passing over the children. They needed men to stay on the ship to keep order. I volunteered. I am sorry I left you, but I saw one young woman - who looked so like you - elbowed out of the way by a fat man in a dinner suit so he could take her place in the lifeboat.'

'No,' gasped the woman.

'There were some acts of great heroism on the *Titanic* that night, but there were also men who showed themselves to be the basest of cowards. You could have come with me. That could have been you. I had to volunteer to stay. You understand, don't you, my love.'

'Oh, Edward!'

'I can feel myself fading, my love. I will be gone soon. I will love you for ever.'

'This is all a bit predictable, is it not,' said Klaus softly to me.

'At least she is giving comfort and good advice,' I whispered back.

Suddenly Madame Arcana's voice shot up several octaves. 'Charlie. Charlie-boy, are you there?'

'I'm here, Charlotte,' said the unremarkable man in a surly sounding voice. 'Autumn sunshine consoles my soul, but my heart aches.'

'Ooh, Charlie-boy.' Madame Arcana giggled. 'You aren't half naughty. Uncle says you need more lead in your pencil. Time to get yourself some oysters. But not the French ones. He says they're the ones that give you the runs.'

Beside me I heard Klaus stifle a giggle. Richenda stiffened indignantly.

'Now, now, Charlotte. There's decent ladies and gents sitting at this table. You mind your manners. I've only come to see that you're doing all right and not looking down on anything you shouldn't.' said the man.

'I keep my peepers shut tight,' said Madame Arcana continuing in the girlish voice. 'I don't know half of what Uncle talks about. I was a good girl. You know that, Charlie-boy. I never crossed a line. That would have been too naughty by half. But I hope you find the right girl, Charlie. One who can look after you proper like. Got the right stuff.'

'That's enough, Charlotte,' growled the man. 'You've taken up enough of these good people's time.'

'He is certainly a believer,' whispered Klaus to me.

'Maybe a regular,' I whispered in return.

'Hmm, yes, she would learn more about him each time,' said Klaus thoughtfully. 'You are most astute, my dear.'

Madame Arcana returned to her normal voice. 'I have another message, but I cannot understand it. Please be patient while I call on my spirit guide. I'm afraid she can be quite a mischievous thing.'

'This gets more interesting,' said Klaus softly but with amusement in his voice.

'Ethel, dear, are you there? Can you help me, dear?'

said Madame Arcana. 'There is an older lady who wants to speak with someone here, but I cannot understand her.'

'Maybe she has forgotten to put her teeth in?' whispered Klaus.

'I'm busy,' said Madame Arcana in a perfect rendition of a spoilt eight-year-old. 'I want to play with my dollies.'

'Now, dear, you have all the time in the world to play with your dollies. I only need your help for a moment. The older lady is getting very agitated,' said Madame Arcana.

'It's mean to say I have all the time in the world,' she answered in the child's voice. 'I'm not in the world anymore. I'm…'

Madame Arcana cut in with her normal voice, 'Don't be difficult, Ethel, or I won't use you again and you know how you like having someone to play with.'

'Oh, I suppose so. She doesn't like being referred to as old, but she looks like she died at a hundred and ten. Her face is all wrinkled like an elephant's backside. She says her name is Alexandria. Alexandria Von something. Bitter?'

'It cannot be! My grandmother was Baroness Alexandria Von Ritter,' said Klaus to me.

'It's one of those foreign names,' said Ethel. 'She smells of mothballs and lavender.'

'Lieber Gott. Es ist meine Oma. Ich bin hier, Grossmutter.'

'She says her great-grandsons are in danger.'

'Peter und Heinrich?'

'She's nodding. She says she sees them walking along a road. There's a black cloud ahead. It reaches all the way down to the ground. They're walking towards it. They're walking slowly. They don't want to be walking this path. They know there's something bad inside the cloud. They don't want to go there, but - they must? I don't understand why they don't go another way?'

'Wo ist?' said Klaus.

'She says the cloud is big, very big. It's the darkest storm she's ever seen. It frightens her. It frightens a lot of people. It's a bad, bad thing. She says Peter and Heinrich mustn't go into the cloud. If they do they'll die, but if the storm arrives, they'll have no choice. I'm frightened, Madame Arcana. The old lady is scary. I won't talk to her any more. She's talking faster and faster now. I can't keep up.'

'But I must know more,' cried Klaus, reverting to English. 'Little girl, I must know what threatens my sons.'

'I won't look. I won't,' said Ethel. 'It's too horrid. Far too horrid.' Then Madame Arcana slumped forward on the table.

'What do we do?' cried Richenda.

'I think we should stay still as she asked,' I said calmly.

'You're right, miss,' said the unremarkable man. 'I've seen this before. She'll be back in a moment.'

Beside me I could sense Klaus was deeply disturbed.

Madame Arcana raised her head. 'I am sorry,' she said. 'Ethel can be unruly. She is difficult to work with and I am tiring.'

'But no one has spoken to me yet,' said Richenda.

'Sometimes the spirits do not have a message no matter how much we wish they did,' said Madame Arcana, weariness sounding in her voice.

'But I have a serious issue,' said Richenda. 'I need guidance.'

Madame Arcana bowed her head. 'I will try once more. But I warn you, I cannot make the spirits speak. It is as they wish.' She took several deep breaths. 'Is there anybody there, who wants to speak to anybody here?'

Then, suddenly, as if he were in the room with us, I heard my father's voice issue from Madame Arcana's lips. 'He's a good man,' he said. I felt a tear trickle down my face. My throat was too dry to speak. I understood he was giving his blessing for my marriage to Bertram. A great peace descended on me. My father had been a wise and compassionate man. I believed that even alive he had had the ability to see into the hearts of men. If he thought Bertram a good man, I could be assured I had made the right choice.

Madame Arcana slumped onto the table once more. Her hair tumbled down. When she lifted her head, she appeared most dishevelled. 'I am spent,' she said in a voice of utter weariness. 'I can do no more. You may break the circle. I am done.'

Tempted though I was to stay and aid Madame Arcana, I realised I could not give away my connection without undoing all the work she had put into convincing Klaus of the dangers of war. At least, this is how I interpreted her storm clouds, though whether he would do the same remained to seen. The unremarkable man turned up the lamps, so I could more clearly see the medium. She sat back in her chair, half-heartedly pinning up her fallen hair. She had gone so pale her rouge stood out on her cheeks like a doll's face. I hoped she had not travelled here alone. I rose with the others and exited. Outside the tent we immediately divided up into groups. The young couple disappeared quickly, still holding hands, but talking in a most animated way. The unremarkable man, at some point, exited. I did not mark when. The fish-smelling woman nodded at Richenda and me and gave us a slight smile. She wandered away into the main hall like a woman in a daze.

Klaus' aide came over to him and bowed as he snapped his heels together.

'I believe we are now due to meet the rest of the delegation in the dining pavilion, sir.'

'Ah, Friedrich, was that not a marvel? I arrived as a sceptic, as my young friend will attest.' He nodded to me. 'But I depart a believer.'

'I am afraid I cannot join you in your belief, sir,' said the aide, looking hard at me. It struck me that it would be more natural for him to speak in German and I wondered why he was allowing me to understand their conversation, but then he turned and spoke directly to me. 'What did you think, Fraulein?'

I smiled. 'I must admit to being undecided. I have seen Madame Arcana perform, if that is the word, twice before. It has often struck me that her spirits hand out the most sensible advice, but as to their verisimilitude, I can only say that I have heard no one challenge her.'

'I assume, like others in her profession, that she used no person's name before they gave it to her?' said the aide in near perfect English. The word 'profession' was said with a palatable dose of cynicism.

'But she named my grandmother and my sons,' objected Klaus. 'I certainly did not volunteer that information.'

I looked from one to the other. 'I think you will find that your aide - I presume that is your position, sir - will point out that you are a person of note. In other words, that the medium may have asked the attendants here who was in the delegation. Did you join the performance by chance or was it pre-planned?'

'Two of us were scheduled to attend,' said Klaus. 'Mein Gott! We actually drew lots to see who would attend. I could have missed this marvel if it was not for the chance that fortune favoured me. Unless you wish to suggest one of our countrymen is in league with Madame Arcana, Friedrich? And what would be the point? She is paid regardless of her comments.'

'She does have a reputation to maintain,' I said, before this Friedrich could point out she might have gathered information about all the delegation. I grew certain he was the German equivalent of a Fitzroy, and I thought I should do my best to reinforce this part of Fitzroy's cascade. I therefore decided to play a flawed devil's advocate. 'If a guest goes away unsatisfied then I assume it would affect further bookings. You are obviously a man of significance. She would not want to offend you.'

'You make my point for me,' said Klaus, as I had hoped, 'It would be ruinous to her career to give me a false message. Why, she even said Grossmutter smelt of mothballs and lavender.'

'Do not most older ladies?' said the aide.

'Bah, you insult me,' said Klaus. 'It was not mothballs the child smelled but my grandmother's signature scent.' He paused and closed his eyes. 'I can remember it as if it were yesterday. It was sharp and sickly sweet. Her first husband had commissioned it for her. When he died she wore it constantly in memory of him. It was perfectly foul. Mothballs would be an easy mistake. I assume the base of the perfume was some kind of distillation from tar. Her first husband was an entrepreneur, but not a very successful one.'

'You appear to have an understanding of chemical science, sir,' I said. Klaus waved my hand away.

'An amateur interest. No more. But it is conclusive evidence that the medium is real.'

I noted Richenda a little way off trying to attract my attention. 'I fear I must say goodbye, sirs. My companion is waiting on me.'

'I would be interested to know what you make of the message for the Baron, Fraulein. Do you have any particular thoughts?' said the aide. He frowned as he spoke, and I could see suspicion written across his face.

'I fear it made little sense to me. If it had been a storm at sea perhaps I could see danger. But why should a storm threaten two healthy men?'

Klaus suddenly clasped my arm. 'You have targeted upon the truth. Both of my sons have aspirations to join the navy. This must be the warning.'

'I could not say,' I said, fearing I had accidentally come too near the intended message by accident. 'But I must attend my friend. I hope you both enjoy the rest of your time in London.' I offered my hand to shake, but Klaus took it and kissed it. I rejoiced that fashion dictated I wear gloves. This Baron was becoming all too familiar and, as Bertram would have said, 'warm' towards me. I withdrew my hand, nodded at the aide, doubtless making him dislike me further, and retreated to Richenda. 'Let us move on,' I said. 'I appear to have become an object of interest to the Baron!'

Richenda regarded me with tear-filled eyes. 'You heard Madame Arcana, she said Richard is a changed man.'

I looked at her blankly.

'Don't you see, the last message was intended for me. My prayers have been answered. My twin has reformed!'

Chapter Six
Amy Causes Chaos and Fitzroy Puts His Foot Down

I had no words to respond to Richenda's extraordinary announcement. I knew her well enough that if she decided something was her prize she would not give it up. I stood no chance of convincing her that the voice had belonged to my own father and he had been talking about an altogether different gentleman. She had heard what she wanted to hear and accepted it as a fact. I bundled her in the direction of where I hoped to find Bertram. I would need his help in undoing this mess.

But we had only started in the direction of the more mechanical section of the exhibition when Bertram came running towards us. His face was red, and he muttered a stream of excuses as he pushed past other visitors in a manner most unlike him. He stopped in front of us. He was breathing so heavily speech was difficult.

'Good heavens, Bertram,' said Richenda, 'you sound like a steam train. What exhibit can have caused you so much excitement? Have the Germans found some miraculous way to drain watery land?' She gave a little chuckle, in no way concerned for her younger brother's state. I, on the other hand, knowing Bertram's heart condition and perhaps valuing him more highly than his self-obsessed sister, attempted to lead him to a chair. He refused to be budged but bent forward in an attempt to regain his breath. I leaned over too and attempted to catch his words.

'Amy?' I said after listening to him puff for a few moments. He nodded vigorously.

'Oh no,' cried Richenda. 'Is she hurt?'

Bertram shook his head.

'Oh, for heaven's sake, stand up properly, Bertram, and tell me what is happening,' demanded Richenda.

Bertram did his best to comply. 'Tree,' he managed to pant.

'Did he say tree?' said Richenda. 'He must have gone mad. I am so sorry for you, Euphemia.'

Bertram shook his head firmly. Then winced and went rather green around the gills.

'No, there are trees in the pavilion,' I said. 'I read about it before we came.'

'How extraordinary,' said Richenda, still not grasping the heart of the matter.

'Richenda,' I said, 'does Amy know how to climb trees?'

An expression of enlightenment dawned on Richenda's face. It told me all I needed to know.

'Where?' I said to Bertram. He pointed.

'Look after him,' I commanded Richenda and lifted my skirts almost to my ankles as I ran off in the direction indicated.

'But I am her mother,' I heard Richenda say behind me. However, a diet largely composed of cake has its effects and I quickly left her behind. I had to trust that Bertram would have the sense to wait and recover before he followed us. Obviously, Amy had not responded to his command or was unable to come down out of the tree. She will respond to me, I thought. Even in my own head I heard those words in my mother's voice.

I turned the corner into one of the wider areas of the

Pavilion and above the heads of a small crowd I saw the tree. Amidst its still green leaves shone the bright red curls of Amy. She was sitting astride a branch. Every few moments she put something from her pocket in her mouth, took it out and threw it down below. I could not see what or where because of the distance between us. 'Excuse me. Let me through,' I said a dozen or more times as I forced my way towards the foot of the tree. There I found Rory.

'I cannae make the lassie obey me, Euphemia,' he said. At that moment another small missile rained down upon his head. He caught it in his hand and showed me. 'Half-sucked sweeties, the disgusting wee brat.'

'Can she get down on her own, do you think?' I asked. 'Or should I find someone to procure a ladder?'

'If the way she got up there is any sign,' said Rory, 'I would say she would have no trouble coming down it she wants to. Went up like a squirrel with a cat behind it.' He looked up at her. 'Amy Muller, you stop that and get down here this instant!'

Behind us, among the now substantial crowd who had gathered to watch this live amusement, I heard mutterings of 'Of course she is German' and 'No English girl would ever behave like that.' There were also comments of 'Hoyden!', 'Tomboy!', and 'Apeish!'. But it was the ones about her nationality that bothered me most. Here was Fitzroy attempting to do his best to bolster relations between Germany and the British Empire and Amy, in her own way, was souring this.

'Get down here this instant,' repeated Rory. If I have learned anything from my mother, it is that one issues neither commands nor threats more than once. If you have to do so, then you have lost.

'You'll have to go up and get her,' I said to Rory. He

sighed and began to strip off his jacket.

'It would have to be my good suit,' he said. He handed his neatly folded jacket to me. 'Either you come down, young lady, or I'm coming up,' he shouted up at Amy.

Where upon Amy pulled her masterstroke. 'You are not my papa,' she screamed at the top of her voice. 'Leave me alone! I want Papa.'

At this point an official-looking man with fearsome side whiskers made his way through the crowd, loudly demanding passage. I guessed him to be someone who was primarily employed to ensure visitors stayed the right distance from the exhibitions and to discreetly point ladies in the direction of the powder room when asked. However, this situation appeared to be all his dreams come true. In a loud, and not particularly refined accent, he called to the crowd to stand back and give him room. 'Nothing to be concerned about 'ere, ladies and gentlemen. I am an employee of Crystal Palace and I have the situation under control. There is no need for panic.' Up to this point there had been much murmurings and curiosity, but not, as far as I could see, any panic. However now the crowd had been asked not to panic, they began to get restive and wilful, as if wondering if there was something worth panicking over after all. Above all, the thirty or so people gathered showed no sign of moving. If anything, more people were joining them. A buzz of asides and whispered comments hung ominously over the crowd. I looked up and caught Amy's eye. She grinned, the little minx. Then the official addressed her, 'Is this 'ere man bothering you, young lady?' His voice carried to the back of the crowd who, as one, pricked up their ears. Amy squeezed out a couple of tears and adopted a lisp.

'He wanth me to come down, but I don't wanth to,

officer.'

Calling the official an officer did Amy no harm in the man's eyes. He adopted an avuncular, if still uncomfortably loud tone, 'There, there my dear. No one will harm you while I am here. You can come down.'

'But I am thcared,' lisped Amy. I mentally ran through the punishments my mother had allotted me in her time and decided that none were harsh enough.

The bewhiskered official turned to Rory, whose pale skin had turned an unfortunate hue. I would not have said he was blushing, because Rory would never allow himself to show such emotion in full public view, but his colour was certainly heightened. 'So, am I to take it you are related to the young lady, sir?'

Rory's deep voice with its Scottish burr was all too audible as he replied, 'Not exactly.' I am sure he had a good and clear explanation to follow that would have defused the situation if it were not for another official, almost the twin of the first, arriving on the scene. As he pushed his way unceremoniously through the crowd he called, 'You 'avin' trouble there, Alf?'

'This 'ere man seems to have chased this young girl up one of our trees,' responded the first official. 'It's not looking good for you, sir,' he added to Rory.

Rory pulled himself up to his full height and began, 'Now see here, my man…' But Alf's reinforcement had now got to the front of the crowd and to everyone's amazement he rugby-tackled Rory. Although much shorter than Rory, he was somewhat rotund and had the element of surprise. Rory went down like a felled tree. I was some feet away, but I heard the audible outrush of air as Rory had the wind knocked out of him. The official went down on top of him and he disappeared from my view. I pushed my way to the front of the line in time to see the two men entangled. At that moment Rory drew up his legs and kicked out, sending the official flying. Any thought of calming the situation quickly vanished from my head as I found a large man in a blue uniform hurtling in my general direction. I instinctively attempted to dodge and managed to avoid the full force of the official careering in my direction. He still clipped me, but my sideways trajectory made it possible for several good-natured people in the crowd to catch me before I completely tumbled to the floor. My hat went over my eyes and I lost my view. What appeared to be a friendly couple helped me to my feet and guided me to a chair at the side of the chamber. I fixed my hat as well as I could, and Fitzroy's face appeared suddenly very close to mine. I gave a little squeak of surprise. Behind him I could hear what I unfortunately knew to be the sounds of a brawl breaking out.

'That child is hell-spawn,' said Fitzroy so softly only I heard. He then turned and murmured thanks to the closest of my rescuers, leading them to believe I was his responsibility.

'What did you say?' I protested, attempting to rise. Fitzroy took my arm in a vice-like grip and began to escort me away from the scene.

'That you are my wife and of a nervous disposition. You need air, or you will faint.' He added in an undertone, 'Don't protest. I have already indicated you have a disposition to hysteria and you don't want me to slap you, do you?'

'But I have to go back and help,' I said, pulling uselessly against him. For a man who did not appear very muscular, his strength was shockingly iron-like.

'That girl has already drawn too much attention to your

party. You and I, and I hope your beloved swain, will at least escape public notice if I have my way. Don't fight me over this, Euphemia. I am more than capable of picking you up and carrying you out of here.'

'But that would defeat your object of avoiding public notice,' I said through gritted teeth.

'Perhaps,' said Fitzroy. 'But your soon-to-be relatives are providing a fine show.' He grinned at me. 'Besides, you know how I feel about losing - to anyone.'

We were far enough away from the tree now that I knew either a full-scale brawl would be afoot, or the situation would be sorted before I could get back there - even if I could manage to free myself. I capitulated and allowed my captor to lead me outside. Though I confess one of my motivations was purely self-centred. Fitzroy vibrated with anger and I did not want to be the one upon whom his ire became vented.

Once out in the fresh air, he strode quickly down an incline and out of sight of the building, still towing me behind him. By the time we stopped by a park bench I could hardly breathe. Fitzroy had not even broken a sweat. 'Living with the Mullers has made you lazy, Euphemia. Tell me, does your maid have trouble lacing you into that corset?'

I sat down and sought my handkerchief up my sleeve. I had sprinkled it with lavender water before we left. I mopped my brow. 'Don't divert your anger to me,' I said waspishly. 'It was not my intention to come here and it certainly wasn't my idea to bring Amy. At least not without some means of restraint.'

Fitzroy's frown lightened slightly. 'Such as a straitjacket?' he said.

'Nothing short of clapping her in irons,' I said. 'Poor

Rory.'

The frown descended once more. 'He handled matters badly.'

'He isn't a nursemaid,' I said.

'You're very keen to defend him,' said Fitzroy. 'I wonder how Bertram would feel if he knew that?'

'What?' I said and scowled back at him.

'Does he know you were once engaged to Rory?'

'It's hardly a secret,' I said. 'He is not pleased but it was a long time ago.'

'But does he fully appreciate what the two of you got up to?' said Fitzroy.

I stood up. 'Stop right there,' I said. 'If I ever aid you again it will be for the sake of my country and not because you think you can somehow blackmail me into assisting you. I will not bow to such dastardly intimidation.'

Fitzroy gave a crack of laughter. 'That's my Euphemia,' he said. 'Thank you. I rather like being called dastardly. Do you think I should grow my moustache longer and wax it to be worthy of the title?'

'Oh,' I said. 'You're just trying to keep me from going back inside.'

Fitzroy nodded. 'I suppose I was also testing to see how open you are to the notion of being blackmailed. As I have informed you before, I am not a gentleman.'

'No, you are not,' I said with feeling.

'I should imagine it's all over by now. I am sorry to say, Euphemia, that my money is on Amy, not Rory. It would not surprise me to learn he was in the back of a police van on his way to jail.'

'You need not sound so pleased about it.'

'I am not. I could have used him,' said Fitzroy. 'Did you notice that when Rory addressed Amy, he used her full name? If things had gone against her, the crowd may decide to indulge in some anti-German feeling, which on today of all days would not suit my purposes. Needing to spring Rory from a jail cell would be infinity preferable to having to deal with the discomfort of the German delegation. Speaking of which, I have learnt that you were most helpful in convincing Klaus of the truth of Madame Arcana's vision.'

'Really,' I said, taking the opportunity to sit down again as Fitzroy seemed to be in an unusually chatty mood. 'I tried very hard not to be convincing.'

'Exactly,' said Fitzroy, leaning against the back of the park bench as if we were the closest of friends, 'And, thereby, convinced him much more than if you had told him you believed in it. Well judged, Euphemia. I knew I could count on you.'

'More than I can say for Madame Arcana. Her impression of my father might have been well meant, but it inadvertently convinced Richenda that her brother, who arranged this gathering, has turned over a new leaf.'

'What? She cannot be that stupid?' said Fitzroy. 'What did Arcana say? I did not brief her on a message for you. Do you think I am turning sentimental?'

I frowned. 'No, I agree, that does not fit. Perhaps it was merely a kindness she intended. It is not the first time she has impersonated my father.'

Fitzroy's face showed what I took to be genuine surprise. 'I shall have to speak with her. I do not like my operatives to be…' he paused.

'Friends?' I suggested.

'Intertwined,' said Fitzroy. 'Although I long ago accepted with you that Rory and Bertram came along as part of a package.'

75

I blushed fiercely.

Fitzroy gazed up at a passing cloud. 'Although I always knew you'd chose Bertram in the end. Rory is even more flawed than I.'

Before I could reply to this extraordinary statement Fitzroy interjected, 'And there is the very man.'

I saw his gaze had fallen in the direction of the Palace. There, descending the slope at a speed that surprised me, came a figure in dark clothing. Fitzroy's eyes must be much better than mine, for I only realised it was Bertram some moments later. My shoulders released tension I hardly knew I had been carrying when I saw him. Being alone with Fitzroy is always trying.

'Gosh,' said Bertram on reaching us, 'that slope is jolly deceptive. I had no idea it was so steep until I started down it. It's small wonder no one uses this path. I can imagine all the dowagers tripping over their tiny dogs and going head over heels in a flurry of petticoats and paws.' I giggled at this image. Fitzroy merely raised an eyebrow. He had sunk back into being enigmatic and sardonic - his favourite demeanour.

'What happened?' I asked. 'And how did you know where to find us?'

Bertram panted slightly. 'Forgive me for answering in reverse, my dear. Fitzroy arranged this meeting with me earlier today while you were in with Madame Arcana. Was it informative?'

'I'll tell you later,' I said. 'Tell me about Rory and Amy.'

'Rory, Amy and Richenda,' said Bertram, with the air of one about to embark on a long tale. 'Do you know, she uses withdrawal of cake as a punishment. It seems most effective. Anyway, Amy was up this tree…'

'The resolution, if you please,' said Fitzroy. 'Some of us are on the King's shilling.'

'The tree is fine, everyone else is a bit battered.'

'A little more,' said Fitzroy, his voice tightening.

'Something of a scuffle broke out. McLeod's got a black eye and has been banned from the Palace for life. One of the officials got his nose bloodied. The other left the scene limping and clutching his - er - personal parts. Richenda sent Amy back in a cab with McLeod to the hotel. The police managed to calm the situation. A couple of Red Cross volunteers soothed the nerves of various ladies. The tea shop gave out free tea. For the most part I think the women got their men under control. There's a lot of talk about it, of course, being a little German girl that caused all the trouble, and Richenda is going around explaining to everyone how Amy is no more German than she is despite her name. Or at least she was until I bought her an enormous slice of cake and promised to go and find you, Euphemia.'

Fitzroy leaned forward. I caught a whiff of his cologne, spicy and masculine. I also saw first-hand the weariness etched on his face. 'What on earth possessed the child?'

'Ah, well, that's the really interesting part. She said a nice gentleman gave her a tuppence to play a trick on McLeod. She said she'd run away from McLeod because he only wanted to look at boring things and refused to buy her sweets, when she came across this nice gentleman who asked her why she was on her own. She explained she was stuck with her uncle's servant and what a boring old sheep he was, and he came up with the tree idea. She said she wasn't sure, but the nice gentleman gave her tuppence for sweeties, so she thought she should. Apparently, he said McLeod had once worked for him and it would do 'old starched trousers' good to have a prank played on him.'

'Richard,' I said.

'Do you think?' said Bertram. 'I did wonder. Sounds like the kind of thing he'd do. Always was a spiteful child. Used to lock me in a cupboard so I missed tea when we were young. Used to eat my share of the buns.' The memory of this indignity caused my beloved to frown deeply.

'I suppose that's where Richenda got the idea to lock me in a cupboard, before she got away from him.' I said.

'Do stop your babbling,' snapped Fitzroy. 'Can you not see the danger all of you, even the child, were in?'

'He's a nasty man, I'll grant you,' said Bertram. 'But he wouldn't hurt a child, would he?'

'He makes the majority of his income from manufacturing weapons of war,' said Fitzroy. 'Who do you think they are designed to hurt?'

'Well, soldiers,' said Bertram. 'I grant you that's bad.'

'Bertram, I believe Fitzroy is saying that Richard does not care who he hurts. He is an unscrupulous man, who will use anyone to his advantage.'

Bertram glanced at Fitzroy. 'I suppose it takes one to know one,' he said.

Fitzroy laughed. 'Touché, Mr Stapleford. But I, at least, am on the side of the angels.'

I was only half listening to them. 'So, I take it that an injured Rory, Merry, Amy and two babies are now alone at our hotel suite?'

'She brought the babies here?' snapped Fitzroy, for once showing some humanity. 'Has Muller lost all control over her?'

'Yes,' said Bertram. 'And no, we didn't know until it was too late. We informed Hans at once.'

'Then you had better hope he has sent people to your hotel,' said Fitzroy.

'Why?' said Bertram.

'Because otherwise,' I interjected, 'the children, Merry and McLeod are in the utmost danger.'

'You don't think that Richard would...' said Bertram.

'Kidnap them?' said Fitzroy. 'Set the whole damn place on fire? I would not dare to predict what injury he would contemplate. He is as unpredictable as he is evil.'

'I cannot understand his intentions,' I said. 'It is all muddled to me.'

'That is because you believe him to be acting on only one agenda whereas it seems he is attempting to fulfil two objectives at once,' said Fitzroy. 'His main objective will be to unsettle the German delegation and undermine our efforts at making peace. Richard would make far less money in peacetime.'

'The devil,' said Bertram under his breath.

'Also, gathering you in London gives him the chance of taking out all the children at once. I take it he is somehow behind the whole trip.' I nodded. 'It is one of the signs of his insanity,' continued Fitzroy, 'that he is determined to own Stapleford Hall himself. So far, his new bride shows no sign of obliging him with an heir. So regardless of what may be agreed legally, Richard is not one to take any chances. He intends to remove any rivals to his own future children.'

'We must go back to the hotel at once,' I said to Bertram. I rose to my feet, as did Fitzroy.

'I am genuinely sorry,' said the spy, 'But I cannot allow you to do so.'

Chapter Seven
Falling for The Enemy

'What the devil do you mean?' cried Bertram.

I curled my hands into fists. My nails cut into my palms. I truly wanted to strike Fitzroy. 'He means, Bertram, that he needs our help to smooth over any difficulties with the German delegation. He will say our duty is to our country first and as it was your, and my soon-to-be family, we must help him. He will enforce this by saying that hundreds of thousands of lives hang in the balance.'

'Not quite, Euphemia,' said Fitzroy. He took a full hunter watch from his pocket and flicked open the lid. 'The German and British delegation are currently at lunch and, for the time being, I believe them to be in no immediate danger. I chose and vetted the caterers. There are too many people around - they are dining in the Palace's central dining hall - for anyone to interfere. However, this afternoon they will be dispatched in smaller groups around the Palace for the final leg of their tour.'

'You must have men on site,' said Bertram.

'There are diplomatic aides from both sides present, but on our side, at least, there are no other counter-intelligence agents. I need to arrange for back-up and it is not as easy as a simple telephone call.'

'Should you not have thought of this before?' said Bertram. 'It is not our problem. It is yours. Euphemia and I are civilians.'

'Civilian assets,' said Fitzroy. 'Perhaps I should have

foreseen this. But I researched thoroughly the delegates who were being dispatched from Germany. I have only this morning discovered there has been a substitution.'

'How does this affect us?' said Bertram.

'He is pro-war, isn't he? This substitute,' I said.

'I am afraid so, Euphemia,' said Fitzroy. 'And the man he is accompanying is the man we chose to target for the cascade.'

'Klaus?' I said. 'You mean that supercilious aide of his, Friedrich?'

'I have now received information that Friedrich has been sent by the pro-war faction in Germany to counter any British sympathies. How far he is prepared to go to achieve his aim I cannot say.'

'You cannot expect Euphemia to put herself in the way of an assassin,' exclaimed Bertram. 'That is no work for a lady.'

'Some of the best assassins in history, and more recently of my personal acquaintance, have been women.' said Fitzroy.

'Stop trying to distract me,' said Bertram. 'I will not allow Euphemia to do this.'

Fitzroy raised an eyebrow and looked from Bertram to me.

'I do not believe Eric here is asking us to place ourselves physically between the assassin and his target. Rather that we keep Baron Klaus Von Ritter from being alone with this Friedrich. You used the word assassin, Bertram, not Fitzroy. This man may only mean to expose the exploits that Fitzroy has planned for what they are - a set of tricks.'

'You make me sound like a parlour magician,' said Fitzroy in a wounded voice.

Bertram ignored him. 'It's clear Fitzroy has lost control of the situation and needs someone to stand in. He said this man is here to counter any schemes to make the Baron look unfavourably on war. Well, if he is an arms dealer himself, or anything like my own brother, I can tell you there would no scheme that he would not stoop to. You are correct, he did not use the word assassin. He does not want to frighten us off. He would never tell us that, but I would lay odds that it is exactly what this Friedrich is.'

I looked at Fitzroy. 'What do you know of him?'

'Not very much. He joined the party so late our informants have not been able to come up with much. This could mean one of many things. I am not inclined to guess.'

'You mean he could be some kind of counter-intelligence agent, who is so good as his job you have never heard of him?' I said.

'Or an assassin,' said Bertram.

'Yes, Bertram, or an assassin. He could equally be an arms dealer or a war sympathiser who was the only one who could be added to the party at the last minute. What happened to the man he replaced?'

'Ah, well,' said Fitzroy. 'That all seems a bit unfortunate.'

'Oh, here we go,' said Bertram. 'He was murdered, wasn't he? The assassin's first target.'

'We have no actual confirmation that the replaced man was murdered.'

'But he is dead, is he not?' I said.

'Fell under the wheels of a carriage. It happens more often than you might think,' said Fitzroy.

'Bah!' said Bertram, rudely, throwing up his hands and walking off a few steps.

I turned to Fitzroy. 'I understand you are in a difficult position. Do you really have no other assets in the field?'

Fitzroy shook his head very slightly.

'The other man at Madame Arcana's séance?'

'You are most acute,' said Fitzroy. 'I cannot locate him.'

'His body is probably hidden under a tea trolley,' said Bertram tartly.

'He works for Edward, not me,' said Fitzroy referring to the head of his brother agency, who concentrated on internal matters for the sovereign. 'He does not need to answer to me for his whereabouts, but…'

'But under the circumstance you might have expected him to say he was leaving?' I said. 'Perhaps he has had the same idea as you and has gone to arrange help?'

'Perhaps,' said Fitzroy. 'I do not know, but I cannot count on it.'

'Send Euphemia,' broke in Bertram, striding back into our midst. 'You and I, Fitzroy, we can deal with this fellow while she gets reinforcements.'

'It is too difficult and too complex to explain to Euphemia how to signal…' Fitzroy broke off. He appeared to age before my eyes. I noticed how lacking in colour his skin had become, and had he always had so many lines on his face? His eyes looked past me into some dark place. 'If I had an alternative, do you not think I would use it?' His voice sounded dull and hollow, quite unlike his normally robust self. 'We are at the last chance. A last chance that is barely a sliver of hope and upon which rests the lives of so many.'

'Of course we will help,' I said quietly. 'We have no option. The stakes are too high. However, I fail to see what we can do, except to keep the Baron in public places. I have some slight acquaintance and I imagine I might construe a situation. But I sensed from him that he was not averse to the company of young ladies and I would need to tread carefully. If I could keep him occupied for up to half an hour, perhaps Bertram could then construct some ruse to divert him for some time longer. I take it we are competing against what he believes to be his schedule, so we will need to be either more pressing or more entertaining to attract his attention.'

'Yes,' said Fitzroy.

'Yes what?' said Bertram.

'Yes, to everything your intelligent fiancée said.' He flicked open his watch again. 'I estimate you have ten minutes before they leave the dining room. You will need to move fast.'

I knew Bertram well enough to know he could continue to argue the point for hours. He prefers any plans to be detailed and well thought out. So do I, but I am more prone to thinking on my feet than my beloved. I assume this ability arises from the necessary skills I had to invent to keep the Staplefords from learning my real identity over the past three years. I nodded to Fitzroy, gathered my skirts in a modest fashion, but one that allowed me to move at more than the gentle pace normally preferred by ladies, and headed off up the path to the Crystal Palace. In my peripheral vision I saw Fitzroy turn and move away at a speed that was just short of a sprint. Bertram made bleating sounds some way behind me, but in a few moments, I knew he would follow.

I already had the Palace in my sights by the time he caught up. Having been of the gentry all his life, he is less fit than I. Beads of perspiration clung to his forehead. 'You know we would have had to agree in the end?' I said.

'And time was of the essence, so I merely moved things forward.'

Bertram, who does he best to be fair, puffed, blew and harrumphed before agreeing reluctantly with me. 'But what do we do?'

'I am going to make him take me to tea,' I said.

'The man will have just this very moment finished eating.'

'I know,' I said, 'but I have an idea I believe will work. I suggest you hang back and when he finally gets up from the table, that's when you step in and talk to him.'

'About what?' said Bertram.

'I do not know,' I said. 'What do gentlemen discuss? Fly fishing? Horse racing? Probably best not to discuss foreign affairs, but are there not many kinds of sports that you could refer to?'

'I do not know what German gentlemen do for sport,' said Bertram, sounding flustered. 'This is too bad of Fitzroy. He could have told us more about the Baron.'

'Maybe he would have if you had not been quite so argumentative,' I said.

'Well, pardon me for trying to be protective of my beloved,' said Bertram in anything but a loving voice.

'I know he is married with two sons.'

'You seem to know more than one might have thought from such a brief acquaintance at a séance. You also referred to him as liking the company of young women. Are you suggesting this man is a cad, Euphemia? Because if that is the case, I forbid you…'

I stopped and turned. In as icy a voice as I could summon I said, 'I think you should stop right there, Bertram. Things are as they are. I will intercept him, and you will watch from a distance. Should there be any need I am sure you can intercede should you feel I need rescuing.' I placed as much sarcastic emphasis on the last word as I could muster, but Bertram was clearly only half listening.

'I will never be out of hailing distance,' he said. 'Be careful.'

'Good gracious,' I said. 'I am going to drink tea with the man, not follow him down a dark alley.' Bertram gave me a look of discomfort that could have been consternation or constipation. I had no time to enquire. As soon as we came into full sight of Crystal Palace I did not want anyone to be able to see us together. I walked quickly ahead, leaving my annoyed swain simmering behind me.

To be fair, in my time I had got myself into some sticky wickets. The time that I almost ended up as a worker in a bordello sprang annoyingly to mind. But this time, inside England's greatest and most public glass box of a building, surely I could not get into too much trouble?

Once inside, I flashed my ticket quickly at the guard, who frowned slightly at me. It was Alf, who now had his arm in a sling, but I knew I had not announced myself as connected to the child in the tree even if I had been around shortly before the fight kicked off. I gave him a bright smile and marched up to the board near the entrance that had a detailed plan of the layout of the exhibition. It was complicated enough that I ended up tracing the shortest path to the dining area with my gloved finger. Fortunately, the milling throngs had somewhat thinned due to the luncheon hour and no one appeared to observe me. I then headed off as swiftly as I thought I could without attracting undue attention. Close to the dining area was a ladies' powder room. I quickly entered and, finding it empty, was able to make the adjustments required.

I emerged in time to see the German delegation leaving the area. A gentleman with a ramrod-stiff back and formidably puffy white sideburns now led the group. I thought it most likely he was a retired military man and wondered if Fitzroy had done due diligence in checking those who had been chosen to show off the exhibition. He looked for all the world to me like someone who would have fought in the Second Boer War. Towards the back of the group I spied my target. At this point I very much wanted to look round and check that Bertram had, as he had promised, remained within hailing distance, but I knew to do so might well give me away. I spied Friedrich, bending close to Klaus and whispering in his ear. I needed to act. I walked forward, slightly unsteadily and a few feet from the Baron and his aide, let out a soft, but well-pitched, 'Ooh,' as I slumped to the floor. I mentally crossed my fingers that Bertram would guess my ruse and not coming running to my side.

I heard a man's voice cry out, 'Good Lord! Look at that!' I kept my eyes tightly shut and listened to a flurry of male indecision as to what to do with a fainted woman. One man said loudly, 'I will get a vase from the table. A good dash of water will set her to rights.' I heard his footsteps running off. It took a lot of willpower not to open my eyes at that moment. Still, I reasoned, a woman suddenly shocked into wakefulness with cold water might be forgiven for striking out. Since the incident with the police rider at the suffragette march I had become aware that I had retained the strength of my working days and could exercise it at a pinch, even if in a slightly haphazard manner. Really, I should get Fitzroy to give me boxing lessons.

Before the running man could come back I heard

Klaus' voice. 'But I know this female. You must not be dashing water on her. She is a lady. Friedrich, be of aid, and help me get her to her feet. Major Green, pull over that chair.'

I felt hands upon my person. Some were of greater use than others. Two strong hands in particular went under my arms and hoisted me up. They came so close to certain areas of my chest that I had to force myself not to flinch. Instead I let my eyelids flutter and parted my lips to utter some soft, feminine sounds. I was deposited with reasonable gentleness into a hard chair. 'Not that, you fool,' said Klaus. 'Fetch her a glass of water. Or brandy. Brandy would be best.'

A breeze wafted across my face. I opened my eyes fully to see the efficient Friedrich waving a folding newspaper in my face. Klaus half knelt beside me.

'Your face whiteness is coming away,' said Friedrich.

Well, I thought, I had not allowed for someone to blow a storm in my face with his newspaper. I said, 'Oh, how embarrassing. I had thought to give myself some colour after I had washed my face, but...' My speech was strung out and breathy. 'It is so hot in here,' I ended and sagged somewhat in my chair.

'Take this dear,' said a gruff voice. The whiskered man handed me a glass of brandy. I took it in a limp hold. However, Klaus placed his hand around mine, so I could not accidentally spill the wretched stuff. 'You must drink, Fraulein,' he said. 'It will do you good.' I slowly sipped the nasty stuff and immediately coughed and spluttered. Friedrich stepped back. 'The Fraulein is recovering. We should move on.'

'Yes. Yes. I am afraid we are on a tight schedule,' said Major Green, pulling at his side-whiskers. 'Are you here with someone, young lady?' I nodded with what I hoped appeared great effort. I also winced. Despite my best efforts, my head had collided a little too firmly with the floor and I could feel a bruise forming. Another skill I would need Fitzroy to teach me.

'Lady Stapleford,' I said using the old, and incorrect, manner with which Richenda had liked to be addressed. Her brother having gained the title on their father's death, and she being his twin, could not be persuaded for some time from incorrectly using a title herself. Of course, when she married Hans, he had cut short such pretensions. However, I felt if I had a slight concussion I could be forgiven for using her old name.

'Send a page to find Lady Stapleford,' commanded Green and Friedrich as one. It made me think Friedrich remained in the military. The rest of the gentlemen, without ladies to guide them, were as inept as I had suspected when faced with a fainting woman.

'You can leave,' said Friedrich to the others. 'I will notify a guard and he will keep an eye on her until her companion appears. We need waste no more time on this distraction.' I heard a rumble of satisfaction break out among the gentlemen. I did not think them unfeeling. I knew they would be desperate to get away from a potentially embarrassing sort of situation. The Germans were no doubt wondering what kind of lady I was to succumb in such a manner and the Englishmen were horrified that one of their ladies should yield to heat. After all, we owned India and those of us out there were legendary in their stout-heartedness.

'I will stay with her until her friend appears,' said Klaus, exactly as I had hoped. 'I will catch you up.'

'But it is important we complete the tour,' objected

Friedrich. 'It would be an insult to our hosts.'

'I think it would be more insulting to leave one of their ladies alone in such distress,' said Klaus.

'Then leave one of them to tend to her,' said Friedrich softly but acerbically to Klaus. 'This is not our business, sir.'

'She is a nice lady and I know her,' said Klaus quietly back. 'I will not leave her with a stranger. It will only take a few minutes. Go with them, Friedrich. You can take notes. You're a sharp boy.' It was a clear and polite dismissal. The delegates continued to mill around muttering to each other, not unlike pigeons, I thought, who had discovered there was no one around to throw them seed. I reached up and touched the side of my head. I flinched at my own touch, but my hand did not come away wet with blood.

'I think I may need some ice,' I said. I heard my voice shake slightly. By this point I genuinely felt unwell.

'We shall go back into the dining room,' said Klaus.

'I do not want to cause a fuss,' I said. 'Perhaps the tea shop. It is smaller and more out of the general way.' Also, I knew the dining room would be getting a cleaning down and setting up for supper. Although less central, the tea shop would provide for a better flow of disinterested passers-by. 'Can you walk?' asked Klaus.

'Of course,' I said standing too quickly and having to sit down again almost at once. 'In a moment.'

'Go on, the rest of you,' said Klaus. 'This lady is an acquaintance of mine. I will catch up with you later. My aide will fully update me.'

Major Green threw me a worried look, but quickly corralled his troops and led them off, with Friedrich almost walking backwards in his efforts to keep his eyes on us until the last possible minute.

I stood again. This time I felt more stable. 'Take my arm, Fraulein,' said Klaus and I did so gratefully. The Baron must have studied the floor plan of Crystal Palace for he led me carefully but unerringly to the tea shop. Once he had seated me and asked for some tea, he hailed a page and relayed to him to direct Lady Stapleford to our new location.

The tea, when it came, was piping hot and very strong. Klaus insisted on heaping mine with sugar. 'I am sure you have a most sweet nature, but the sugar will do you good. My father had an interest in medicine and he swore that the intake of sweet tea increased not only the chance of a patient's recovery, but the speed of it too.'

I sipped my tea. 'Your father was a doctor?'

Klaus shook his head. 'He would have liked to have been, but the position my grandmother married into made that impossible. He had many estates to oversee, but he kept his interests alive as well as he could, as I do mine.'

'I am sorry I interrupted your tour,' I said.

'It was not that interesting to be honest,' said Klaus. 'The Major he was trying to add - what would you call it - zest to his conversation, but unfortunately someone enquired at dinner if he had seen action.'

'Ah,' I said. 'He would have been of the right age to be in the Second Boer War. Those who served in it seem only too keen to speak of their experiences.'

Klaus shrugged. 'War is neither heroic or romantic. It can be necessary, but I find tales of adventure like the Major's difficult to enjoy.'

'Well, from the little I understand we lost shockingly at the start. The South African Republic and the Orange Free State only became the single nation of South Africa in

1910.' I smiled lightly. 'My father liked me to read him current events from the newspaper. His eyes failed towards the end.'

'That is sad,' said Klaus.

'Perhaps,' I said, 'soldiers like Major Green like to dwell on the successes in the hope that others will forget about the failures.'

Klaus tapped me playfully on the hand. 'You are wise beyond your years, my dear. It is the way of most men to focus on their achievements and forget other less pleasant truths about their past. That is why we need smart, intelligent women like yourself to keep us in line.'

The conversation seemed to have tipped into an intimacy that I had not expected. I liked Klaus, but although he sat a decent distance from me, it remained the very edge of a respectable distance and I felt that any moment he might decide to breach my defences. I steeled myself to repel him. I did not think he would grab me or any such crudity, but in his eyes I saw an intense light of interest. He leaned in towards me. Now, only inches remained between us. 'My dear,' he began.

'Oh, there you are!' cried a familiar voice. 'Why on earth did you ask them to look for me using my old name? It quite took me by surprise. I thought they were hailing my mother!' Richenda threw herself down into a chair. 'Is that tea hot? Goodness, after such a shock I need cake and plenty of it.' She registered Klaus' presence fully. 'For medicinal purposes,' she added. 'My doctor says I need feeding up. I recently gave my husband twins.' She preened slightly at this and then frowned.

'This is your companion?' said Klaus. The pitch of his voice rose, and his eyebrows shot up. A moment later he appeared to have composed himself. I glanced at

Richenda. She had already got the attention of a waiter and was instructing him to bring a large - yes large - plate of cakes, and ones with plenty of cream and not the scrapings the English tea rooms normally offered. The dead birds on her hat jiggled as she did so, and her ample bosom heaved under its many layers. The fact that her dress was outlandish, out-modish and comprised of vividly clashing colours barely drew my attention any more, but for a moment I saw her through Klaus' eyes. I determined, for Hans' sake, that Glanville and I would have to attack and thin her wardrobe. We could always blame moths.

I nodded. I genuinely could not think of the right words to explain our relationship. It was complex enough to make the merge of two states seem trivial.

'Then I will leave you in her care?' said Klaus. He coloured slightly. He had clearly meant his words to come out as a statement and not a question.

I looked past him to see Bertram hanging back against the wall. I smiled at Klaus. 'I will be fine. You must rejoin your tour. You have been more than gracious.'

Klaus stood and taking my hand, kissed it. At the same time, he bowed and snapped his heels together. 'It has been my honour. Might I hope you will be in the metropolis some day? I would be delighted to call upon and ascertain that you have sustained no serious hurt.'

I hesitated. I wore an engagement ring. I hoped this would be enough to keep our relationship within polite etiquette and, really, I could see no way to deny him his request without seeming rude. 'I am staying at the Carlton,' I said. 'If you ask at the reception desk for Euphemia St John they will notify me that you are present.'

'Excellent,' said Klaus, who had still not released my

hand. 'And we will take tea in their Palm Court. I hear it is very fine. I look forward to it.'

He kissed my hand once more and finally let go. I smiled again and gave a slight nod. Really, I did not want to encourage him any further. As he turned I caught sight of Bertram; he was already moving to intercept the Baron, but he did not look happy. Then Richenda turned her attention to me and began to babble about Amy and Rory and how servants today were not up to the job. She further complained that in arranging to send Rory and Amy off in a cab to the hotel, a waiter had come and removed her plate of cakes. 'And do you know, they did not even offer to replace them?'

'How terrible,' I said. 'Most inconsiderate.' My mind rested half only on her conversation. I angled my chair under pretence of avoiding the direct sunlight to gain me a better view of Bertram and Klaus.

'I suspect it was a German waiter,' said Richenda loudly. 'I expect we young English ladies all look the same to him.' A waiter deposited a three-tiered rack of cakes in front of her. 'Thank you,' said Richenda. 'Where is the tea?'

'But, madam, you only ordered the cakes.'

'How can one possibly eat cake without tea!' responded Richenda. I leaned back in my chair to try and hear what Bertram was saying.

'That may be, Herman. We met at Baggy's little place up north. Fly-fishing? Got three of the biggest whoppers I have ever seen.' Bertram's accent had become positively cut glass and his mannerism aped the foolishness of the late, but unmourned, 'Baggy' Tipton.[5] I found myself quite

---

[5] Please consult my journal *A Death in the Wedding Party*

proud of him. I did not know he was able to act so well. He spoke very fast and the Baron was floundering deeper and deeper in confusion.

'Which kind of tea would madam prefer, we have…'

'China tea. I want China tea. I want a large pot and fresh cups for myself and my companion. Euphemia, do you want some cakes too?'

I had to bring my attention back to table and my eyes met those of the startled waiter. 'But these are cakes for two, madam.'

'Well, that is just ridiculous…' Richenda begin a long diatribe on how ladies who had recently given birth needed extra calories. I shuffled back and switched my attention to Bertram. I didn't know how long he could keep his ruse going and I needed to be able to step up again if necessary. Although all I could think of was fainting again and with my luck if I did so the Baron would insist on accompanying me back to the hotel. It would get him out of the way of the danger Fitzroy feared. However, I had the feeling it might well imperil my virtue to be alone in a cab with Klaus Von Ritter.

I was delighted to hear that Bertram was still going, all guns blazing. He ran through a series of events at which the two of them might have met: Lord's cricket grounds, a reception at the Palace,[6] a musical festival in Austria. The list went on and on as Bertram played to perfection the giddy idiot who is absolutely sure he has met someone before and will not let the matter rest. The fact that he insisted on addressing Klaus as Herman made it all the more difficult for the Baron to escape. When he proclaimed his real name, Bertram took it as a great joke.

---

[6]The *other* Palace.

'You're such a card, Herman! So where *was* it we last met? For the life of me I cannot recall, but I am not letting you get away. I will remember in a minute. You're not getting one over on old Georgie!'

'Who is old Georgie?'

'George. Like the king!'

Klaus, still trying to remain polite for the sake of Anglo-German relationships, was becoming so flustered his English understanding was slipping.

'God save the King!' said Bertram with a foolish giggle. ''And all that. What do you say we find somewhere to have a snifter and chew the rag?'

At this point something inside Klaus snapped. 'I do not know you,' he roared. 'I never before seen you in my life have. I do not want the rag to chew or to you have a snifter!'

'I say, old chap,' said Bertram in a hurt voice. 'Are you really not Herman the German? Was up at Oxford with my brother Oliver?'

Drawing himself up to his full height and speaking slowly and carefully as one might to an idiot, Klaus said with anger throbbing in his voice, 'I am not, and I have never been Herman the German. I have never been up Oxford! If this is your idea of some foolish prank…'

Bertram began to babble apologies. He was extensive and profuse. He begged for pardon more frequently than he had claimed to know Herman. He began to offer to show Mr Ritter London. 'Whatever you want to see, old chap. I know all the sights and I can get you into some damn fine shows and clubs. Whatever you like.'

Poor Klaus simply could not get away. His colour rose, and I began to fear he might succumb to a heart attack. In the meantime, I tuned back to Richenda in case I needed to contribute to the conversation to avoid suspicion. My fears were groundless. She related some story of meeting up with old school friends. One of them had been accompanied by her grown-up daughter. 'Her skin! You should have seen it, Euphemia. It looked like the cloth Glanville uses to dust my shoes. No one would ever believe we were in the same year. Her with her eighteen-year-old daughter, a gaunt, simpering little thing with about as much femininity to her as a park railing. She looked every inch a *grandmother* and she had the audacity to say about me having the babies...' Clearly, she needed no more from me and I did not wish to interrupt her flow.

Then Klaus bowed and snapped his heels together. Bertram managed to block his exit, but Klaus only bowed and snapped his heels together more loudly. Either Bertram would end up wrestling the man to the ground in a bear hug or he was going to have to let him to escape. I twisted and placed my hand on the back of my chair, so I could rise with speed to my feet should I need to act.

'So anyway, I said I would meet Richard here. He is ten minutes late. Just like him,' said Richenda. My attention snapped back to Richenda.

'Richard is meeting you here?' I said. I felt as if I actually had been drenched with water from the vase on our table. 'Here? Now?'

'Euphemia! Have you not been listening to a word I said?'

Yet another time in my life when I could not tell the truth. Honestly, my father brought me up never to lie. Since meeting the Staplefords, I have broken this rule more often than I have drunk tea and I am an Englishwoman through and through. 'I fainted earlier,' I said. 'I hit my head quite hard on the ground. Perhaps it has affected my hearing.'

'Gosh,' said Richenda. 'I wondered why you had me paged. I thought that German fellow was bothering you.' She cocked her head on one side. 'Your hair does look a little crushed on the left side.'

'That is the side I fell on,' I said. I half rose. I could see Klaus walking determinedly past Bertram, but at the very moment Bertram would have needed to tackle him to the ground to keep his attention, Fitzroy emerged into the lobby and made a beeline for Klaus. Bertram withdrew with a heavy heave of his chest, visible even from this range, as he sighed with relief. I sank back into my seat. Richenda was still talking. 'Won't your cake be getting soggy?' I said. 'You did ask for extra cream.'

Expressions flowed like a river in full stream across Richenda's face. Her jaw dropped, her mouth opened, she lowered her brows and finally her eyes bulged out. Cake won out. She reached for the largest meringue, filled with cream, and wedged as much as she could into her mouth. The outer shell shattered sending shards of sugar across her bosom and a significant portion of the table. Cream bulged out of the sides of her mouth. Her eyes filled with horror. She grabbed her napkin and hid her face behind it. Chewing, gulping and a slight choking sound came from behind the linen. Bertram came and sat down beside me. 'If I never have to do that again I certainly won't mind,' he said.

'I listened to as much as I could,' I responded, 'and I thought you magnificent.'

Bertram smiled. 'It was all I could do not to rush to your side when I saw you fall. I take it that was deliberate, and you are unhurt.' His eyes searched my face for reassurance. My face met his. For a moment there was only the two of us in the entire world. Unconsciously we shifted forward in our seats, inching ourselves towards each other. His hand reached out to my arm. I believe I may have given a little sigh or some such indication of happiness.

'Euphemia,' said Bertram tenderly.

'BUURRRP!' uttered Richenda.

The magic ended as we tumbled heavily back to reality. Bertram shot back in his seat as if pulled by a thousand ropes. I felt my face flush so red I thought my hat might catch fire. I do believe this is the closest I ever came in my entire career to kissing in a public space. For all I am a woman now, my mother would have had me beaten with a broom.

Richenda emerged sheepishly from behind her napkin. 'Good gracious,' she said. 'Wherever did that noise come from?'

I turned to Bertram. 'She's meeting Richard here. Now.'

'The rotter's already ten minutes late,' said Richenda attempting to draw our attention to Richard's shortcomings rather than her own digestive ones.

Bertram sprang to his feet. He grabbed my hand and pulled me up. For a moment I thought he would pull me into his arms. I confess, remembering our earlier lost moment, I would not have resisted. But he did not. 'Dear God, do you realise what that means, Euphemia?'

'That he needs a new pocket watch?' said Richenda.

I looked into Bertram's paled face and the realisation dawned on me. 'He has no intention of meeting her.'

'He bloody well better,' said his twin. 'I did not come all the way to the metropolis and alienate my husband only to be stood up.'

We both ignored her. 'It's a ruse,' I said.

Bertram nodded. Neither of us spoke another word, we were too busy running for a cab.

Chapter Eight
The Worst is Realised

Fortunately, there had been an influx of visitors for the afternoon and, therefore, a lot of cabs were looking for return fairs into town. Bertram and I leaped into one, bypassing the queue.

'Oi!' complained the cabbie.

'Three guineas,' yelled Bertram. 'To get as to the Carlton Hotel in one piece as quickly as you can.'

'Right-o, governor,' said the cabbie and cracked his whip.

We were both thrown back against the cushions as the cab lurched into motion. Bertram put his arm around my waist to stop me falling and conveniently forgot to remove it.

'You think he is after the children?' I said.

'I fear so,' said Bertram. 'I keep telling myself he will only hold them as ransom until the necessary legal documents are signed.'

'But there is an easier way for him to be sure,' I said quietly. The horses' hooves thundered over the cobbled road. 'No,' I said my voice fading below the clatter. 'He would not.'

Bertram took my face in his free hand and turned it towards him. 'He is an evil man, Euphemia. He has got away with murder once.'

'But babies!' I cried. 'How could he?'

'He is not made like you and I,' said Bertram, 'But let us hope we are both wrong.'

'We should have known,' I said. 'We…'

'No,' said Bertram cutting me off in as firm a tone as I had ever heard him use, 'you cannot blame yourself. There is only one villain in this piece.'

'Amy!' I cried with relief.

'Termagant that she is, I doubt she could overpower whoever he has sent,' said Bertram.

'No,' I said almost crying with relief, 'She was sent back to the hotel with Rory. He only has to hold out until we get there. There is hope.'

Bertram rammed with his cane at the roof. 'Another guinea,' he cried. 'If you can go faster!' I doubted the cabbie could hear us, but his ear must have been attuned for such offers, for the carriage nearly reared. Then it rocked and swayed with such force that no conversation was possible, and I feared I would lose my breakfast. The images in the windows were no more than blurs. Bertram hung grimly onto the strap with one arm and onto me with the other. We were both bounced and jostled to the extent I feared there would not be enough witch hazel in the city to calm our bruises.

Finally, we lurched to a stop outside the Carlton. Bertram flung open the door and kicked down the step. He jumped out and held out his hand to me. I took it and wobbled. I more fell than exited the carriage, but I landed on my feet. 'Doorman will pay,' yelled Bertram and sprinted up the steps still holding my hand.

We heard the cabbie cry out behind us. Neither of us paid him any heed. We pelted across the lobby, causing dowagers to drop their pince-nez in their laps and snatch up their little dogs in protest. Bellboys and footmen weaved out of our way. Onward Bertram and I ran. I had my skirts in one hand and my ankles felt a breeze upon them. I caught sight of more than one monocle falling from its moorings, and at least one child cried something inappropriate at us as we dashed past, only for their governess to box their ears. We arrived at the lift and demanded our floor.

Then we had to stand still as it rose up. Both of us leant heavily against the walls. My breath laboured. My heart grew sore enough I thought it might burst. I glanced at Bertram. His face had greyed, but he shook his head at my look of concern. Neither of us spoke. We knew that once the elevator stopped we would be sprinting again.

It stopped. Leaving the un-tipped bellboy with nothing more than disappointment, we launched ourselves towards the Stapleford suite. Bertram stopped at the door. He rummaged frantically in his trouser pockets 'Do you have your key?' he panted. 'Rory has mine.'

I didn't bother answering. I had seen what I feared most. I pushed lightly against the door and it swung open. The lock had been broken. Bertram gasped in horror. 'No,' he whispered, and in that whisper was the echo of a thousand nightmares come to pass.

I stepped forward, but he caught me. 'Let me go first,' he said. 'We do not know what is to be found.' I opened my mouth to protest, but Bertram spoke first. 'There is no sound of conflict, Euphemia. Whatever has happened has happened.'

I let him go. I sank down into a heap on the polished marble floor, tears streaming down my face, and prayed and prayed and prayed.

What felt like an eon later, I felt Bertram's hand under my arm. How I knew it was him I could not say, but I knew before I looked. 'It is not the worst,' he said. 'It is bad, but it is not the worst.'

Inside the suite a sorry scene met my eyes. Furniture

lay overturned. Broken glass and shattered crockery littered the fine carpet. One small settle had been righted. On it lay Rory. Blood covered his shirt. The skin around his eyes had swollen so much they were no longer visible. 'It's his nose,' said Bertram. 'I think it's broken. He's breathing. I found him sprawled on the ground. He gave them a good fight.'

'Where are the children?' I asked.

'Not here,' said Bertram. 'That's what I meant when I said it's not the worst. They've taken them.'

'But…'

'And they've taken Merry. Do you see what that means?'

I shook my head. I could barely take in what was happening. I knew Richard to be vile beyond measure, but I had never dreamed he would hurt infants.

Bertram took me by the shoulders and gave me a little shake. 'Euphemia. Euphemia. Listen. It means they needed someone to look after the children. They would hardly take Merry with them if they were planning the worst. You can bet that Merry did not make it easy for them. You know what a firecracker she is.'

I gave a slight smile. 'She would have fought them tooth and nail.'

'Exactly,' said Bertram. 'It would have been far easier for them to knock her out and leave her behind than to get her out of the hotel.'

'But how did they do that?' I protested. 'How?'

'That's what I am off to discover,' said Bertram. 'It might have been a service lift, or maybe they held a knife to her, under a coat or something, so she wouldn't protest.' He ignored my cry of horror. 'Either way, there has to be a trail. I have to go now. If there is any chance of catching them I will leave a message with reception to call you.'

'I will come with you,' I said.

'You need to look after him,' said Bertram, indicating Rory. 'We cannot leave him. He may need medical attention.'

'I'll call reception. They can send someone,' I said.

'For now, Euphemia, it may be best to keep this between us.' He looked into my eyes and I saw a thousand fears. I nodded.

'Come back to me,' I said and surprised him with a quick kiss. He responded with passion, then tore himself away, leaving me with the unconscious Rory.

I checked again that Rory was still breathing. Then I went to the bathroom and wet a small towel. I came back into the room and placed it across his forehead. I realised I needed another towel to clean up the worst of the blood on his face and I repeated the procedure. I moved slowly, as if I was struggling through waist-high mud. Everything was an effort and took so long it felt as if time had begun to flow backward. I dabbed ineffectively at the blood on Rory's face. Eventually I thought to get a basin of hot water and continued wiping gently around his mouth and nose. I opened his sodden shirt and saw the blood had gone through to his vest. I pulled at the shirt sleeves, but I could not remove any clothing while he lay on his back. He was too heavy to move. As I dabbed the towel around his nose he gave a little moan. The sound reassured me of life, but I wondered if it really was broken. I ran my finger lightly down it and found an unnatural bump. I had the thought of searching through Glanville and Merry's possessions. In Glanville's I found some smelling salts and in Merry's some bandages. I thought of calling down to reception for a doctor, but Bertram had yet to return. It could be that I would imperil the children further if I drew attention to the scene. We were yet to hear of any ransom demand.

Taking a deep breath, I put my fingers along the sides of Rory's nose and then, on a count of three, I straightened it. I did not need to use the smelling salts.

Rory's eyes flew open and he sat up sharply, swinging out with his left fist. I ducked.

'It's only me,' I said. 'Your nose was crooked. I straightened it.'

Rory made a strange noise between a gurgle and a growl and flopped back against the cushions. 'Euphemia,' he said. His voice sounded strange. I offered the bandage to him. He put up a hand to his face and felt his nose. He winced. 'Give me a hand up,' he said. I did my best, but I could barely steady him as he made his way to the bathroom. He peered through his swollen eyes at his reflection for a moment. Then he tore his shirt and dropped it on the floor. He did likewise with his vest. 'At least I wasn't wearing my jacket,' he said. He looked down at his trousers and swore when he saw the speckles of blood on them. He peered at himself in the mirror once more.

'I take it you and the cavalry came back just in time,' he said.

'No,' I replied.

Rory swayed and gripped the edge of the wash basin to steady himself. 'You mean the children are...' I watched the colour drain from his face.

'Are gone,' I said. 'As is Merry. We are expecting a ransom demand.'

'How long?'

'I don't know. We came back as soon as we realised Richard had drawn Richenda away. You were unconscious when we found you. Bertram put you on the settle before he ran off to see if he can trace their escape route.'

'Have the police been called?'

'No,' I said. 'Richenda does not even know yet. I believe she is still at the Crystal Palace tea shop eating cake.' My voice broke on the last two words and tears ran silently down my face. 'Should I send her a telegram? It seems so terrible she does not know what has happened.'

Rory suddenly hunched over the basin and vomited. I rubbed his back, but an impatient gesture indicated I should leave him. I pulled the door to but did not close it. I knew it was not uncommon for sufferers of concussion to vomit and then pass out, subsequently choking on their own bile. I listened to hear if he fell, but I only heard repeated retching. It went on for some time. I sat down and watched the door. I told myself the longer Bertram took to return, the greater the chance of him tracing the kidnappers. An evil little voice at the back of my head whispered that it also meant he too might be lying hurt somewhere, or even dead. I sniffed but was determined not to give in to emotion. Once Rory had finished in the bathroom I would need to watch him and then I would need to deal with whatever news Bertram brought back. It struck me then that there was no sign of Glanville. Had Hans' curse of accidentally hiring nefarious servants struck again? Could she have aided the kidnappers? If not, where was she? Surely, they had no use for a lady's maid? Could she be, even now, en route to fetch Richenda or even the police?

Thoughts whirled in my head. I could reach no conclusions and Rory remained occupied. Then I became aware of another sound. It had been in the background for a while, but it was only now I identified it. It was the sound of muffled crying.

Immediately I sprang up. I ran from room to room, but I could see no one. I even looked out of the windows to see if someone was hanging from the ledge, but with no success. I came back to the settle where I had first heard it and stood still, willing my heart to calm within my chest, so I could hear beyond my own heartbeat. Finally, I understood the direction. I opened the door of the sitting room cabinet and there, squashed up among the bottles, was a sobbing Amy. I pulled her out and into my arms. She clung to me and cried as if her heart would break.

I comforted her as best I could. I hugged her, smoothed her hair and told her she was safe. But it was only when Rory came, somewhat shakily, back into the room that she responded. She broke out of my arms and ran to him. He staggered backwards under her assault but managed to keep them both upright as he caught her in an embrace. Then he picked her up and carried her to the settle. He sat down himself, with obvious relief, and pulled her onto his lap.

'She hid in there,' I said, pointing to the cabinet.

'Clever girl,' said Rory. 'I told her to hide when I heard them at the lock. They did not even try to see if the suite was unlocked but jemmied the door with a crowbar. I managed to disarm the first man of that, but the second one stepped over the first and hit me so hard in the face I saw stars. After that, it is all a blur. I threw punches and they hit me. They were skilled fighters. I was in a brawl or two in my younger days, but these men knew what they were doing.'

Amy looked up from Rory's shoulder. 'They spoke funny,' she said. 'I heard them talking after the fight. I listened very hard. I thought they might say something important, but I did not understand a single word. I am sorry,' she said and began crying anew. Rory petted her.

'I did not think they resembled English gentlemen,' said Rory. 'Their suits were not merely cheap but oddly cut.'

'There speaks the valet,' I said attempting to smile.

'Can you remember anything of the funny words they said pet?' Rory asked Amy.

'One of them said "scheisse" a lot,' said Amy.

'German,' said Rory. 'One of the few words I know. A man at the exhibition said it earlier and Bertram told me what it meant.'

'What does it mean?' said Amy.

'It's a bad word, pet,' said Rory. To me he said, 'What do you want to do? Do we wait for Bertram or do we act?'

'Someone must stay with Amy,' I said. 'Where is Glanville?'

'She went shopping,' said Amy. 'She said mummy's stockings were a disgrace.'

'Convenient,' I murmured. Rory caught my gaze and looked a question. 'I had no idea who is involved other than Richard. Or to be honest, even if he is behind this. It could be...' I was about to tell him about Fitzroy calling Bertram and I to action. Could it be that our intervention with Klaus had earned us this terrible revenge?

'Of course it's Richard,' snapped Rory. 'He convinced Amy to play the trick up the tree, so she'd be sent back to the hotel. He wanted all the children together. He didn't count on my coming with her. I am not exactly a nursery maid.'

I nodded. It was the version of events I preferred, cowardly though it was to think this way. Rory broke in on my thoughts again. 'So, do I wait for Bertram?'

111

'You are in no state to go anywhere,' I said. 'You can barely stand up and you may well have a concussion. I will fetch help.'

'No,' said Rory, 'I must at least try to find Bertram if you will not let me go to the police. He may be in trouble.'

Amy clung tightly to Rory. 'Don't leave me,' she begged.

'I am not going to Bertram's aid,' I said. 'I have no indication as to where he might be. I am going to get help. Amy, I need you to stay with Rory. If he gets sleepy you are to pick up the telephone apparatus over there and ask someone from reception to come and help you. This is very important. Do you understand? I need you to look after him.'

This allocation of responsibility worked better than any of my previous attempts to soothe the child. She stopped crying and nodded. 'I will take care of him, Aunt Euphemia.'

'Euphemia,' protested Rory, but I was already half-way to the door.

'Secure the door behind me as best you can,' I commanded. 'We do not know if they will return to look for Amy.' I strode out of the suite as if I knew exactly what I was doing.

Only outside the room did I realise that I had blood on my hands and my dress. I did not have time to go back. Instead I located the servants' stairs – a skill from my below stairs days - and made my way quickly outside. I ran to the nearest cabbie. He took one look at me and shook his head. I took a leaf out of Bertram's book. 'Two guineas if you will take me to Crystal Palace,' I said.

'You're one of 'em suffragettes, ain't you?' said the cabbie. He spat a plug of tobacco on the pavement. 'I ain't havin' any truck with you lot. Get back to the kitchen where you belong.'

'Three,' I said desperately. I had some money on me, but not enough to cover this fare. I reasoned I could always bolt at the other end.

'You got a homemade bomb in that bag of yours?' said the cabbie. 'I should call the coppers on you! Get on with you.'

I moved to the next cabbie, who had overheard. He returned much the same answer, but with expletives. However, the third cabbie took me up. 'It's not a bomb, is it love?' he asked.

'No, I swear on my life I have no such thing, nor any projectiles or anything offensive. Only my coins in my bag,' I said. My despair had brought me to the edge of tears.

''Op in then, darlin'' said this cabbie. 'I don't have any problem with women getting the vote. I've let me wife be one of you lot, just as long as she doesn't get into any trouble. I'm not having any of this "deeds not words" nonsense.'

I thanked him profusely and climbed in. I dared not ask him to go faster in case he thought I was up to some mischief. Instead, during what seemed an interminable journey, I counted out the coins in my purse. I had two and a half guineas and a shilling. However, the carriage turned one corner rather quickly and the shilling escaped my gloved grip and rolled under the seat. I had enough sense not to try to find it in a bouncing carriage. I had no desire to end up in Rory's predicament.

When the carriage drew up outside the Crystal Palace I clambered down. 'I am very sorry,' I said to the cabbie. 'I appear to only have two and a half guineas. There is a further shilling under one of your seats. Will this do?'

'That's a'right, love,' said the man, leaning down to take the coins from me. He smiled showing a gap between his teeth. 'The fare's nowhere near that.' He took only what was necessary. 'That'll do,' he said. 'I don't know what trouble you're in and I don't want to know, but you look like you need the rest.'

I swallowed back sudden tears and thanked him. Then lifting my skirt above my ankles, something which I was becoming all too accustomed to, I ran into the pavilion. The guard on the door let me past. He either remembered me or was uninterested in running. Admittedly, he had already had a day that had been far more active that he must have anticipated when he accepted the position.

I stopped in the middle of the central hall and looked around wildly. For once, luck favoured me. The delegation must have completed another leg of their tour, as they were being herded into the tea shop where I had been taken by Klaus what felt like a lifetime ago. I spotted several waiters buzzing around the delegation. Fitzroy stood further back, observing all, and watching the delegation and their interactions like a hawk. I contemplated a full on confrontation but decided running through the atrium flashing my ankles had been enough of a show. I moved closer to a large potted plant and waited a few moments, so that my breathing slowed and my facial colour returned to normal. I tweaked my blouse and skirt, so that they looked slightly askew, but the blood spots were less evident. Then, moving slowly, I sidled around the edge of the room towards the spy.

Normally I would not expect to have the remotest chance of taking Fitzroy by surprise, but his attention was all on the delegation and on sweeping the room around them for threats. He clearly thought he remained innocuous enough that he would go unnoticed. Or rather that his skills of blending into the background were excellent. If Fitzroy has a failing - and while he may have many personally - as a spy he is excellent, except that he has never been a man of modesty. He did not notice my approach. Behind him I noticed a recess over which the exterior shades had cast their shadow. It would be perfect for my purpose. I crept forward much as I had done when playing Grandmother's Footsteps with little Joe. Only at the last minute did I dive forward, throwing myself at the spy and hurtling us both into the recess. Fitzroy immediately threw me off and pinned me painfully on the ground. I do not think he even recognised it was I until he had me completely at his mercy.

'Euphemia,' he spat quietly and with fury. 'What the devil is the matter with you?'

'Release me,' I gasped with difficulty. He half sat, half lay atop of me. Cold metal pricked my neck and his forearm was across my throat. The touch on my neck withdrew although the area smarted and I could feel a trickle of blood. He eased back, still pinning me, but with his forearm away from my neck. Instead one strong hand held my shoulder in a vice-like grip.

'I could have killed you,' he said. He glanced around. 'I still might. You can thank your God that this area is unpopulated.'

'That's why I chose it,' I said. 'I am not a fool.' Fitzroy raised an eyebrow at that. 'I needed to speak with you urgently.'

'There are easier ways,' he said, still not releasing me. I saw suspicion cloud his eyes. 'Do they have Bertram?'

'Who is they?' I demanded.

'Whoever put you up to this ridiculous escapade. I can think of no other reason why you might risk your life so.'

'I am not under anyone's coercion,' I said, finally grasping his meaning. 'This is my own scheme.' At this both eyebrows rose. 'Richenda's twins and Merry have been kidnapped.'

Fitzroy frowned. 'Merry? Ah yes, your friendly maid.' He shrugged. 'It is nothing to do with me.'

'But I need your help,' I exclaimed. 'After all I have done for -' I got no further.

'You have done nothing for me,' said Fitzroy, his voice like ice. 'All has been done in the name of King and Country.'

Fury overtook me and my voice raised. 'I acted as your executor when you were thought dead...' I had more to say, but Fitzroy clamped his hand over my mouth.

'Be quiet,' he hissed. 'If we are seen I will have to claim you are a militant suffragette and have you taken to jail.' I hoped my eyes blazed with the anger I felt. I certainly willed them to do so. I considered biting his hand, but unlike Bertram or Rory, I knew Fitzroy would have no compunction in slapping me. He leaned close and spoke quietly. 'I regret that Richenda has endangered her children. I wish them no harm. You forget that the scheme to come to Crystal Palace was not of my making. I have no part in this. I am here to protect the interests of our country and I must put that above all else. All else.' He leaned closer, so our faces were mere inches apart, and spoke the final two words with deadly emphasis. 'I now require you to fetch Rory and Bertram and bring them to me. Are they here?' He did not move his hand from my mouth, so I merely shook my head – as much as his grip allowed. 'The hotel?' I nodded. I assumed and hoped that Bertram had by now returned to Rory and Amy.

Fitzroy lowered his mouth to my ear and spoke so quietly that even with his lips almost against my flesh I had to strain to hear him. 'The King is coming here. He has determined to speak to the delegation directly. It is a desperate plan. I am awaiting my reinforcements. I will now need them to prepare for the King. While I do so, I will require you to resume the task of keeping Klaus Von Ritter alive. This is not a job for which I would choose to use amateurs, but I need all my people to prepare the way for the King's safety and security. That must take precedence over all else. Remember the service you pledged when you signed the Official Secrets Act. You may not be an operative, but you are my asset to use as I see fit in the guarding of the security of the country. If, when I remove my hand, you utter one word of protest, I will use all necessary force to incapacitate you and have you removed to a gaol of my choosing.'

He raised his face, so he could look me in the eye. Still speaking quietly, he said, 'If you complete your duties to my satisfaction, I may choose to use my considerable abilities and assets to help you locate the missing children. Do we have an agreement?'

Tears burned in my eyes and one ran from the corner of my eye down across his hand. The expression on Fitzroy's face remained cold and unmoved. I nodded. 'Good girl,' he said. 'That they have taken the maid suggests they are in no immediate danger.' He rose quickly and held out his hand to me. I pettily refused it and scrambled in an ungainly manner to my feet. Fitzroy looked me up and down. 'Change before you return but be swift.' Then he left me. Trembling, I leaned against the glass wall.

Chapter Nine
In Bed With The Devil

'The fiend! I will have his heart for this. I will cut it, still beating, from his living body!' said Bertram when I told him what had occurred.

'But did you find any sign of where the kidnappers went?' I asked. 'How they exited?'

Bertram shook his head. None of us spoke. We were all considering our positions. Bertram paced angrily up and down our hotel sitting room. Rory, now changed into fresh clothing, sat very still in an armchair. The skin round his eyes had reduced in swelling but had gone an inky dark colour. His cheeks were suffused with burgeoning bruises. The way he held himself told me that this might well be the most visible of his injuries. I stood, my hands tightly clasped together so my fingers dug into my flesh, to prevent myself from breaking down and sobbing. I did not know what to do. Amy had been put to bed in the nursery and, after all the commotion, was sleeping as only an exhausted child might.

Eventually Rory spoke. 'Euphemia, are you considering not returning to Fitzroy?'

'Yes,' I said quietly.

Bertram stopped pacing and swung towards me, his face ashen. 'But the King!' he said.

'He does not want us to protect the King,' I said. 'Only the Baron. Who is this Baron against the life of two innocents?'

Bertram came up to me and placed his hand on my

shoulder. 'It will still be treason,' he said. 'But if you determine to follow this course of action,' he swallowed, and I saw how much it cost him to complete his sentence, 'I will aid you.'

I raised my hand to grip his. 'You are everything to me,' I said.

Rory coughed. 'Crushingly romantic as this moment may be for the pair of you, I think you are forgetting that we have no idea where the babies have been taken. Nor, for that matter, by whom.'

Bertram released me and faced him. 'I think we can be certain Richard is behind this.'

Rory shrugged and then winced with the pain of it. 'Most likely, but he did not do this himself. He hired others. Germans, if Amy is correct in what she heard. London is a large city and Richard has deep pockets. We do not have the resources to locate them.'

'You imply Fitzroy does,' I said. The name tasted bitter on my tongue.

'Do you doubt it?' said Rory.

'He would say anything to bend the situation to his will. Do anything, even,' I said.

Rory nodded. 'I agree. He is without scruples. His treatment of you is unforgivable.' He raised his hand before Bertram would begin another tirade. 'But we have never been given reason to doubt that he puts King and Country above all else, have we? In fact, quite the contrary.'

'No, but...' I said.

Rory interrupted me. 'We have to help him. If we do not, the likelihood is we will be in jail long before we can help Merry or the children. We have done many incredible things, Euphemia, but finding one young woman and two small babies hidden in London is beyond us. I hate this as much as you do, but we need Fitzroy's help. And he has clearly laid out the conditions of his aid.'

'He bargains with the twins' lives,' said Bertram in a voice dripping with loathing.

'He does,' said Rory. 'That he has bowed to such tactics that would only make us despise him suggests how much in need of our help he is.'

'I do not believe he cares a fig for our opinion of him,' said Bertram.

'Perhaps not personally,' said Rory, though I thought he was looking overly hard at me, 'but it is easier to get us to do his bidding if we are willing.'

Bertram snorted. 'More flies with honey,' he said.

'He must be desperate,' I said.

Rory nodded. 'I do not believe...'

At that very moment there was the sound of footsteps. 'Whatever has happened to our door!' cried Richenda's voice. She erupted through the door with Glanville on her heels. She glanced around the room, started with horror at Rory's face and then turned to me. 'Where are the children? Tell me they are safe?'

'Amy is asleep in the nursery,' I said.

Richenda sank down into an armchair which creaked under her weight. 'Oh, thank goodness. We have only been burgled. Well done, Rory. I take it you fought them off. I came back from the Palace because I could find none of you - and to my surprise I met Glanville on the steps. She has been buying stockings.' Glanville did indeed have a string-tied brown package in her arms. She had not followed her mistress' lead and sat down. She cast her eyes about the room. An O formed on her lips. Her gaze locked with mine. Her eyes were wide. As Richenda babbled on about the heat of the inside of Crystal Palace and how shocking cab fares had become in London, she spoke over her mistress.

'Where is Merry? Is she with the twins? They cannot be in the nursery if Amy is sleeping.'

Richenda stopped short. She rounded on Glanville to scold her, but seeing the horrified expression on her face, she spun back to me. 'Euphemia?' she said.

'Merry and the twins have been taken,' I said.

'By whom?' said Richenda, frowning. 'Did Hans come? You surely did not fight him, McLeod. I know you have a dislike of one another, but…'

'Richenda,' I said loudly, 'Listen. Amy hid when two men broke into the room. As you guessed, Rory fought them, but had been overcome. While he was unconscious the men took Merry and the twins.'

'Took them? Took them where?'

'Do you not think if we knew that we would be there instead of here?' said Bertram snappily.

'Glanville, do you think you can find the smelling salts?'

Rory reached down by the settle and handed them to her. 'Utterly disgusting,' he murmured. 'I cannae think why any woman would carry these around with her.'

But Richenda swayed in her chair. Her eyelids fluttered and before Glanville could step across the room, she slumped forward. Being inclined to the larger size in certain aspects of the feminine form, she tumbled out of her chair and landed face first on the floor. I noted that neither of the gentlemen had made any effort to catch her. Rory had already taken a beating and so perhaps could have been excused, but Bertram did not stir a hair. I gave him a sour look. He shrugged.

'You may love me for many things,' he said, 'but you must admit my upper body strength is not among my greatest features.'

While he attempted to excuse himself, Glanville fussed over her mistress. She managed to get her upright and leaning against the chair. 'Must have been a washerwoman,' murmured Bertram. 'I hear they have beefy forearms.'

Showing more refinement that my betrothed, Glanville ignored him and placed the smelling salts under Richenda's nose. She came to with a start.[7] She twitched and glanced quickly around the room.

'How? What? Why?' she said in a broken voice and then she burst into tears. Both gentlemen stiffened, and their eyes bulged with apprehension. There is little that disturbs a man more than a woman crying. Especially if he knows her.

'I will telephone to the police, ma'am,' said Glanville. 'How long have the children been missing?'

'Not that long,' said Bertram. 'I ran after them while Euphemia tended to McLeod. I believe we must only have missed them by minutes.'

'Can you be sure?' said Glanville. 'The police will need facts.'

'McLeod was unconscious when we arrived. If he had been out for much longer than that he would be mentally unbalanced. Euphemia?' said Bertram.

'I do not claim any medical knowledge,' I said. 'But my impression was indeed that Rory had only recently passed out. His nose was still bleeding. If it had been longer I imagine it would have clotted. Although when Joe

---

[7]They really do have the vilest smell.

123

broke his nose falling out of the apple tree it did bleed for ages.'

Glanville glanced at Rory. 'Perhaps if we showed them the bloodied shirt they could make an estimation? Or ask a police doctor to do so?'

'Excellent thought,' said Bertram. 'Where did you put it, McLeod?'

I noticed that Richenda's colour had changed from white to greenish. I stepped slightly away. 'Enough, the three of us need to go.'

'What,' said Richenda.

'We think we can find help - special help, but we need to fetch it,' I said.

'Whatever do you mean?' said Glanville.

'Careful,' growled Rory.

'I am afraid I have already said too much. Please trust that we go unwillingly, but we hope to return with help,' I said. Bertram rolled his eyes at me.

Richenda glanced between us. 'What is going on? Is this all your fault?' she said, accusing the three of us.

I reminded myself mentally that these were her twins and the fact she had stupidly brought them to London to visit her completely untrustworthy brother were facts that could be visited later. However, Bertram did not share my opinion and let her have his own unbridled version of his thoughts on her actions. Richenda cried harder. Glanville sat back on her heels.

'I am phoning the police and they will wish to speak to everyone. You cannot leave,' she said in a voice of authority.

Rory pulled on his jacket over his fresh shirt. That he had remained in a state of such undress before ladies and his master spoke volumes of the turbulence within his mind. 'There are some details to which you may not be privy, Glanville,' he said with all the haughtiness a butler might command. 'We must go.'

Glanville shot to her feet and stood between us and the door. 'I do not know what is happening here,' she said, 'But I know my mistress's babies have gone missing and her family wish to quit the scene. That sounds mighty strange to me. You will have to move me bodily out of the way if you wish to pass. Ma'am, you will need to call the police. Can you manage? I will prevent the others from leaving.' Although a mature woman, of not particularly significant stature, she stood legs apart and arms akimbo, in a stance both aggressive and determined. In that moment I realised I rather liked Richenda's lady's maid and I should have paid her more attention.

'Are you sure you want to call the police,' I said as Richenda attempted to pull herself to her feet using the chair. 'They took Merry. I suspect you will shortly hear about a ransom demand. Involving the police at this stage might endanger Merry and the twins. It might make the kidnappers panic.'

'Maybe you should call that husband of yours,' said Rory. 'He is a gentleman of influence. Besides, if you need to raise money, a banker is surely the man to have by your side.'

Richenda and Glanville exchanged glances. 'I will call Hans first,' Richenda said.

'An excellent idea,' I responded. 'He is an intelligent gentleman with a calm and level head.'

'Oh yes,' said Richenda. 'We all know how much you and Hans think of each other.' With this extraordinary statement she went into her chamber were there was a telephone apparatus. The moment the door closed behind her I nodded to Rory. He strode forward and picked Glanville clean off the ground. Bertram and I shot past. We heard Glanville's exclamations of indignation behind us, but we did not look back. Rory joined us moments later in the lift.

'I rather like that wee woman,' he said as the cage descended. 'She has spunk.'

Bertram nodded. 'She is certainly made of the right stuff.'

'I fear Richenda will contact the police,' I said. 'She will be too frightened to telephone through to Hans.'

'Rubbish,' said Bertram. 'He would never lift a finger towards her.'

'I know,' I said. 'But he is a gentleman of - I do not know what the right word is, but I fear he will consider divorce now. Their relationship has never been good. It was passable in the early days, but I think Richenda taking the children to London angered him greatly. That they have been placed in peril because of her actions may be the last straw.'

'A man of set opinions,' said Rory. 'I agree. He is not one to cross and I fear you are right, Richenda has gone too far this time.'

'But the scandal!' said Bertram. 'Divorce!'

'It is not our concern. At least not for the present,' I said as the lift came to a stop. 'I suggest we walk quickly to the cab stand, but do not run. We do not want to attract even more attention to our actions.'

'Agreed,' said Bertram. Then he swallowed. 'I say, McLeod...'

'I have the money for the fare, sir,' said Rory in a distinctly annoyed tone.

'I will pay you it all back,' said Bertram, looking

affronted.

'Oh, come on,' I said. I linked my arm through Bertram's and strode out as much as my skirts allowed for the cab rank.

This time, in the company of obvious gentlemen, and no longer spotted with blood, there was no difficulty in securing a cab. Our cab seemed to travel at an achingly low speed, but now we were working for Fitzroy again we were determined not to draw attention to ourselves. His instructions on that matter had always been firm and clear. Needless to say, we have often flouted them. But now we were to help him protect the King we were all most aware of our duty - or at least I was. I assumed from the sober expressions on the face of the others that they were feeling the same. I was all for telling Fitzroy to go hang himself, but to be asked to help ensure the safety of the sovereign was not something to be taken lightly. I also knew that however strong our determination to find the twins in London, without the help of Fitzroy and his shadowy cohorts, it would prove difficult if not impossible. If, as we thought, it was all a plan of Richard's, then the chances were that Fitzroy had people watching him and his acquaintances. Given reason and opportunity, I hoped Fitzroy would surrender to his darkest nature when finally confronting Richard.

It was with these less than charitable thoughts I occupied myself during the ride. The openness of the cab prevented us from discussing our plans and we sat in silence for the length of the journey. Our peace was only disturbed by the ringing bells of several police cars that passed us. They were not going in the direction of the hotel. But then, I reasoned, the metropolis is unlike the villages I grew up in, and a place of frequent infamy and crime. However, when we got close to Crystal Palace, the traffic slowed to an unendurable pace. Bertram leant his head out the window to demand an explanation, but he brought it back in without saying a word to the driver. 'Traffic is almost at a standstill,' he said. 'Something must be up.'

'Well, if you-know-who has been sighted,' I said. Rory and Bertram both shushed me. 'What?' I exclaimed, 'I could be talking about my mother-in-law.'

'You do not have one yet,' said Rory.

'I am not going to have one,' I said, looking at Bertram, but he appeared lost in thought rather than distraught over his mother.

'I thought the whole point of this excursion,' Bertram soon said, 'was that it was to be kept secret.'

'So did I,' I said. 'But plans do change. The whole thing appeared to have caught *him* on the hop.'

For a moment Bertram looked scandalised until he worked out that the 'him' to whom I was referring was the spy and not the sovereign.

'I think we should get out and walk,' said Rory. 'Even with Euphemia in skirts it will be quicker than the cab the way things stand.'

I glanced out of the window. 'We are very close,' I said. 'I do not object.'

We signalled the cabbie to halt and Rory paid him. While he did so, Bertram whispered in my ear, 'When has McLeod seen you without skirts?'

I started. 'I do not believe he ever has,' I said in some bemusement.

'It was a jolly funny thing for him to say,' said Bertram.

'Indeed,' I said caustically, 'I am still laughing. Honestly, when I think of the things we have on our plate at the moment -'

'I am trying not to think about them,' cut in Bertram. Rory joined us, and we walked quickly towards the common. We had clearly made the right choice as we passed multiple vehicles. The pavements were not crowded as most people stayed in their vehicles. We made good progress. Only as we neared the Palace did we see that all the police vehicles that had sped past us were lined up around the entrance. A cordon of policemen separated the public from the Palace. We could see more than one person on the other side debating with dark-clothed officials.

'They are not letting anyone out,' said Bertram.

'Nor in,' said Rory.

'This could be a problem,' I said. 'What do you think Fitzroy would want us to do? We can hardly announce we are working for him.'

'Perhaps,' said Bertram, visibly brightening, 'the meeting - the BIG meeting - is already underway, and we are not needed.'

'But we still need him to help us find the twins,' I said. 'We have to get inside. You would think the police and diplomats would prefer as small a crowd as possible to deal with while they were on protection duty. It does not make sense for them to prevent people from leaving.'

'Knowing our luck,' said Rory, 'probably something terrible has happened.'

'Do not,' I warned sternly, 'say it. Do not even think of more terrible situations for us to contend with.'

'Not like you to be superstitious, Euphemia,' said Rory.

It was at this point I saw Madame Arcana command the

line of policemen to part as she sailed through. She came directly towards us. There was anguish on her face. We walked quickly, half ran, forward. When we met on the grass of the common, she spoke quietly and with great sorrow. 'He is gone.'

Chapter Ten
The Vanishing Man

'Who?' said Bertram. 'The King? Have we missed him?'

'What do you mean by gone?' said Rory at the same time.

'Kidnapped, but I fear he is dead,' said Madame Arcana.

The world swayed around me. 'Not again,' I said and sunk down with a thud into an unladylike heap on the ground. Bertram hauled me to my feet with difficulty. I did not help. I was a dead weight and near to fainting.

'Tell me we are not talking about the King,' said Rory.

'Good gracious no,' said Madame Arcana. 'The King is not due to attend the exhibition. Wait! Did Eric say he was coming?'

Rory nodded. 'To Euphemia. That is why he sent for us. Not to help with that aspect of it, but to watch over some German aristocracy. A Klaus Von something-or-another.'

'Klaus Von Ritter,' said Madame Arcana. 'It was after his collapse and subsequent death that we noticed Eric's absence. Clearly his murder was a diversion. Eric - Fitzroy - holds some of the key secrets of the kingdom, he will die rather than reveal them.'

'The German is dead? Already?' said Rory in disbelief.

'A hand here, McLeod,' said Bertram, who still struggling with me. I could hear them talking, but it seemed as if their voices came from a long way away. My thoughts, as I took in the situation, were likewise detached from emotion, as if they belonged to someone else. I had liked Klaus well enough, and I had been asked to protect him. It appeared I had failed, and I felt genuine regret - but for Fitzroy too to be dead was unthinkable. He was the only man I could think of who had a chance of defeating Richard and regaining the children.

I heard Bertram say, 'Euphemia is unwell.'

Rory and Madame Arcana appeared to notice my predicament for the first time. Hands helped me to a park bench and I sat down. Someone propped me against an arm. For a moment I feared I had gone blind. When Madame Arcana spoke of Fitzroy's death, my mind had gone back to the grisly search of those bodies recovered by the *Carpathia* I had been forced to endure, searching for his corpse the last time the spy was declared dead. That adventure had ended with him locked in a pigsty awaiting torture and then execution.

I heard Madame Arcana say, 'Oh yes, the poor dear went through a bit of hell last time he died, did she not?'

'Forget Fitzroy,' said Rory. 'Richenda's twin babies have been kidnapped and we need help from your resources to find them. We think Richard Stapleford is involved and the kidnappers are German. We were hoping Fitzroy had kept a watch on him and his associates.'

'Almost certainly,' said Madame Arcana.

'At last some good fortune,' said Bertram. 'So, can we speak with them? Their information may be vital in saving the infants' lives.'

'Only Fitzroy would have known how to contact them,' said Madame Arcana.

'But is there not a back-up plan?' said Bertram. 'I mean, last time he died Euphemia got a letter.'

132

I roused myself to speak. 'Firstly, we do not know he is dead. I have heard nothing more than that he is missing.' I clutched at this hope like a drowning man at a straw. 'Secondly, you mentioned a murder as a distraction. If we can discover who committed this murder, we will be on our way to finding Fitzroy. I agree he is doubtless under interrogation, but it will not be the first time he has borne up under that. Time is of the essence. We should go back inside. Madame, can you arrange that?' As I finished I got to my feet. I had to hold onto the bench to steady myself, but I did not collapse.

Madame Arcana looked me up and down. 'If you are sure. I suggest you take a brisk walk around the common first. No policeman would let a woman who appears to on the verge of fainting in to see a corpse.'

Rory picked up on the implied suggestions. 'Do you mean they do not think he was murdered?'

'The ordinary police? I do not believe so. There will be other investigators on the site, and I imagine Edward has been sent for, but there is no one there I know. Fitzroy was very good at keeping us all compartmentalised.' She saw Rory frown. 'You can only give away the names of the people you actually know about,' she explained.

'Except for Fitzroy,' said Bertram finally catching up. 'He would know everyone. What a prize.'

'Do we think this is the Germans?' I asked.

Madame Arcana spoke, 'We cannot assume anything. The situation diplomatically between England and Germany is at an all-time low, but that is not to say everyone on the German side wishes for war. Nor, for that matter, that everyone on the English side wishes to prevent war. The exhibition may seem like a last dance at the ball for some, but nothing is decided. Until certain matters are set in motion there is always a way back.'

'But if someone wanted war, killing a member of the delegation would be a step towards approaching it,' I said. 'Especially if it was an anti-war campaigner that was killed.'

'Either could be made to work,' said Madame Arcana in such a matter-of-fact voice that I began to see her in a new and harsher light. I had always suspected she worked with Fitzroy gathering and passing information under the guise of her séances. However, I had assumed he had recruited her as an asset, like us, but she spoke with the authority of someone far more invested in what Fitzroy often - obscenely, to my mind - called 'The Great Game'.

'Arms merchants such as Richard have all to gain should war break out,' said Rory darkly.

'Even the threat of war increases profits massively,' said Bertram sadly. 'Some countries believe the more armaments they buy, the better they are prepared to defend themselves. While others buy with the intent of being the aggressors. The problem is that no one ever can tell which is which, and it generally ends badly.'

'For everyone except the arms merchants,' I said. 'Do you think that the kidnapping of Richenda's children was meant to keep us away from Von Ritter, so Richard and his allies could make their move?'

'I do not think any of us are that important,' said Rory.

'There are stages of the game when the most unlikely pawn can become a queen,' said Madame Arcana obscurely. 'If you will excuse me, I shall go and arrange your access. Take Euphemia for that walk.' She made me sound like an inconvenient hound and I found myself blushing. Rory and Bertram hurried to my side to assist me. Madame Arcana vanished.

Bertram noticed first. 'I say, she didn't disappear in a puff of smoke, did she?'

'If I ever had any doubts that she was a fake, they linger no more,' said Rory. 'On the positive side, she is a loyal subject of the crown.'

'Or we presume so,' said Bertram. 'How can we tell she is telling us all the truth?'

'I should not think she is telling us all she knows,' I said. 'She is clearly more important in Fitzroy's network than we are and thus likely knows a lot more. However, if we are to suspect everyone of malicious intent we will get nowhere.' I sighed deeply. 'I want nothing more than to return to the hotel and discover the location of the twins. However, with no leads, our best shot is to investigate Von Ritter's death. We can only hope it leads us to Fitzroy, if not to the mastermind behind the kidnapping of the twins.'

'I don't know,' said Bertram shaking his head. 'Merry kidnapped. The twins kidnapped. Now Fitzroy has been kidnapped. It is as if we have come to London during a kidnapping festival. It cannot all be so coincidental.'

'I agree,' I said. 'Which is what gives me the hope that all these situations are interlinked, and that by untying one knot the rest will follow.'

'I want to believe you are right, Euphemia,' said Rory. 'I do. But it is all…' He did not get to finish his sentence for Bertram gave out a little cry of dismay. 'Look,' he said his voice rising to a squeaky pitch, pointing to the edge of the common. 'Richenda!'

I followed his gaze. 'What? Oh my goodness, he's right,' I said. I could see Richenda in her distinctive costume walking along the edge of the common. She was headed determinedly in the direction of the police cordon. 'She must have followed us. How else would she know we

135

were here? We need to hide. We cannot explain what we are doing!'

Their arms still linked in mine, Rory and Bertram twisted in opposite directions, as they scoured a landscape covered only in scattered trees. It hurt, and I gave an involuntary squeak. Richenda turned towards us and speeded her gait.

'There is nowhere to go,' said Bertram, his voice still high pitched in alarm.

'I dare say we could move faster than her,' said Rory, 'but we cannot get through the cordon until Madame Arcana returns. Unless either of you can think of any way to persuade the police to let us through.'

'We shall have to face her,' I said. My stomach became lead and began to sink slowly to my shoes.

'But we cannot tell her the truth,' said Bertram. 'We are bound on our honour not to.'

'And by the Official Secrets Act,' said Rory. 'We can be hanged as traitors for even disclosing its existence to another soul.'

'That is ridiculous,' said Bertram. 'I shall speak to Fitzroy about this.' Then he recollected our situation. 'When we find him, that is. Honestly,' he sounded most aggrieved, 'it is so inconsiderate of that man to put us in this position.'

'I hardly think he got kidnapped on purpose,' I said. 'No one enjoys being tortured.'

'Probably makes him feel important,' said Bertram crossly. Then he snapped, 'What the devil do we tell her?'

'As much of the truth as we can,' I said.

'We already got close to treason telling her we were going to find friends who could help,' said Rory. 'Be very careful, Euphemia. Richenda Stapleford is not known for

136

keeping her mouth shut. Expect anything you say to be broadcast over the gossip circles within hours.'

'Poor Hans,' I said. 'I wonder if she realises how much trouble she is brewing for him. To be half German at this time is a precarious situation. He needs his wife to be discreet.'

'Then he should not have married my half-sister,' said Bertram. 'Oh, God, here she comes. Stand firm, everyone.' The three of us, arms still interlinked, turned to face her full on.

Richenda stopped in front of us. Her eyes were reddened from tears and her breath caught in her throat. She did not look at us with anger, but with confusion. 'You are on the common,' she said. 'You are not even talking to your friends in the police?'

'We never actually said our friends were in the police,' said Bertram. I kicked him in the shin. He gave me a reproachful look.

'Euphemia, you went for a walk on the common with Bertram and McLeod and left me to deal with the police?' she said. 'What do you think you are doing? Was Richard right about you all those years ago? For the love of God will you not help me find my children?' Still there was no ire in her voice, only puzzlement.

I disengaged myself from the men. 'I know it is hard to understand, Richenda, and it is even harder for us to explain, but we are doing the best we can. We are searching with utmost effort.'

'By walking on the common?'

'We await someone,' I said. 'We will, we hope, shortly be speaking to someone from the police.' This was not a lie as we needed to speak to whoever let us through and to gather as much information as we could about the crime scene.

'Who?' said Richenda. 'Besides, you urged me not to talk to the police.'

As this was true I could not counter it. 'What did Hans say?' Richenda did not reply. Bertram and Rory kept looking towards the Palace clearly hoping Madame Arcana would appear. I, on the other hand, felt certain she would not approach us until Richenda had gone.

Richenda reached into her large handbag. I assumed she was about to produce a handkerchief before breaking into sobs. 'There is a park bench nearby,' I said. 'Let us take a seat.' I attempted to take her arm, but she pulled roughly away from me. She pulled out a folded piece of cloth from her bag and thrust it towards me. 'Look at this,' she said. 'Look.'

I took the cloth. 'Euphemia,' warned Bertram stepping forward, but I ignored him and undid the folds. To my relief no object revealed itself. Instead I saw a wet ruby stain that was in the process of turning to brown.

'Blood,' screeched Richenda. 'You see what they have sent me? Blood!'

'We do not know whose blood it is.' I said careful not to let my emotions show in my voice. 'We do not even know if it is human blood.'

'What else would it be?' screamed Richenda. 'A pig's? That is part of Merry's uniform. They have killed her!' Her voice rose. Cries, halfway between laughs and sobs, broke from her throat. It stunned me. I had seen women pretend to have hysterics before, but never the real thing. Rory and Bertram likewise froze in the face of such extreme emotion. Richenda's cries grew ever louder. Soon we would attract attention. Something had to be done.

It was at this point that Madame Arcana returned. She

slapped Richenda across the face with enough force that the crying woman staggered. 'The grieving mother, I see,' she said to me. 'She is attracting attention.'

'She came with this.' I handed the cloth towards her. 'It is from the nursery maid's uniform.'

'A petty tactic,' said Madame Arcana. 'How do we even know this is her blood? It might be from a chicken or a cat.'

I led Richenda to the nearby park bench. This time she moved without resistance. She wept quietly and without ceasing. I feared she had lost all hope.

'Now, Mrs Muller,' said Madame Arcana, coming to stand over her. 'When did this article arrive?'

After much sniffing and wiping of tears, Richenda managed to say, 'A few minutes after they left.'

'So you caught a cab,' said Madame Arcana. 'Why did you come here?'

'I thought my brother might be here,' said Richenda. I inwardly sighed with relief. She did not suspect our link to the exhibition and the delegation.

'And you were going to ask him for help? Richard Stapleford?' said Madame Arcana.

'Yes. No. I thought he might know where the children were,' said Richenda and began to sob more loudly.

'Where is her lady's maid?' Madame Arcana asked me.

'I expect she left her back at the hotel, in case anyone returned,' I said. Richenda nodded.

'She has some sense then,' said Madame Arcana. She crouched down to speak with Richenda more quietly. 'Your friends are doing everything they can to help you. You must trust them. Was there a ransom note?'

Richenda reached into her bag and produced a crumpled piece of paper. On it I could see written nothing but a very large amount. 'This was in the cloth,' she said.

'Obviously they could not expect you to raise that amount immediately,' said Madame Arcana. 'It will be the first of a series of communications. You would be best served to return to your hotel and let your friends deal with the police. There is nothing you can do here.'

'But Richard!' began Richenda.

'Is not currently in a position to help you,' said Madame Arcana. She beckoned a police constable over. 'See that this lady is returned with speed to her hotel.' Then to us she said, 'Come.'

I tried to convey my sympathy with my eyes to Richenda as I was led away, but she was too occupied crying into her handkerchief to notice me.

Bertram managed to give her a light pat on the shoulder before following the rest of us. 'Buck up, old bean,' he said. 'It will be all right. I promise.'

Madame Arcana led us up to and through the cordon. A few policemen cleared the crowd from our path and we were lead back to the Crystal Palace tea shop. A sign hung from a potted plant declared it closed, but there was a hubbub of activity inside. We walked past the ropes that marked its boundaries and Madame Arcana sat down at a table. She indicated we should join her. 'Until we know exactly how Von Ritter died,' she said, 'I will refrain from offering you tea.'

'Yes, gosh,' said Bertram, who had been eyeing the urn. I could hardly blame him. The last few hours had been extremely unsettling. In such dire situations as these, there is nothing like a good cup of tea to calm one's nerves.

'I am sorry about your niece and nephew,' said Madame Arcana.

'You think the blood was theirs?' I said.

140

'I have no idea, but the kidnapping of these infants is obviously a ruse. The demand for money is way beyond anything Richenda or her husband could ever manage. The bloody dress is meant to frighten. Clearly, whatever is happening, it is important to the kidnappers to keep the three of you off kilter. This suggests to me that your next actions will be vital in our moving forward.'

'So you think the twins are alive?' said Bertram.

'I cannot promise you anything,' said Madame Arcana. 'We are working very much in the dark here. I think the first thing I should get you to do is talk to the police doctor. Perhaps, during my time away, he has discovered something of actual use.' She got up and walked over to the other side of the tea shop. As I watched her passage I spotted a sheet covering a large object on the floor.

'I say,' said Bertram, who must have been following my gaze. 'What do you think that thing is?'

'Von Ritter's body,' said Rory in tones that made it clear he thought the question imbecilic.

I looked from one to the other nervously. The last thing we needed right now was for them to break into one of their bickering sessions. I suspected Madame Arcana's reaction to such would be fearsome.

But the man who came over to the table next was not dressed in a policeman's uniform. It was the nondescript man who had been in Madame Arcana's séance.

Chapter Eleven
The Man Without a Name

'Good afternoon,' said the man. 'I am here to tell you who was observed to be around Baron Von Ritter when he was taken ill.'

'And you are?' said Rory.

The man ignored his question and continued. 'So far the doctor believes that Von Ritter died of a heart attack. As you may have observed he was not a particularly fit man. He was known to dine well and live well. His frame was stocky, and he carried a great deal of weight around his waist. Modern medical opinion would suggest that it was merely a matter of time before he succumbed to his lavish lifestyle. However, shortly after his death, the member of the public who first rushed to his aid, a Dr D.M. Gardener of 14 Brockle Place, observed there was some foaming at the mouth and a distinct smell of almonds. By the time the police doctor had arrived, Von Ritter's aide, Friedrich Gottlieb, a possible asset or operative, had wiped his face clean and tidied the body as much as he could in situ. He opined he had done this for his master's dignity. Here is a list of all the people in the delegation.' He took a list from his pocket and passed it to us. 'Those marked with a cross are, as far as we can tell, the ones who were nearest to him when he died. I suggest you question them first. As far as anyone else is concerned, you are members of the plain clothes police division, who happened to be attending the exhibition. You,' he pointed at Bertram, 'are the inspector and

McLeod is your sergeant. Euphemia is the inspector's wife. Fortunately, she has spent her idle days learning shorthand and is able to assist you. She will not, however, be able to ask questions. She is to function as a secretary.' And with this he slid a small pocket book with attached pencil from his pocket and across the table to me. As he did so, he angled his body to block the action from sight of any of the police milling around the tea shop. If I had any doubts before as to what he was, these were now removed.

'Why us?' said Bertram. 'Surely you have more… more… appropriate people.'

'Instructions were left,' said the man, rising and tipping his hat towards us. 'I will return in one hour at which time you may pose questions to me about any of the suspects you find of interest.'

'Where are you going?' I asked.

'To find information about the suspects of interest, of course,' he said and walked off.

'Do they all have to have that bloody awful sarcastic sense of humour,' said Bertram bitterly.

'We should look at the list,' said Rory.

I opened it out on the table, so we could all see it at once.

Friedrich Gottlieb – Aide to Von Ritter
Dietrich Habermann – German Diplomat
Rudolf Beiersdorf – German Industry Magnate
Robert Draper – British Industry Magnate
Algernon Porter – British Diplomat

'I take it that we interpret "Arms Merchant" when they say "Industry Magnate"?' said Rory sourly.

'We need to talk to them,' said Bertram.

144

Rory and I looked at him in amazement.

'What did you think we were going to do with them?' said Rory.

'I mean,' said Bertram, 'why should they speak with us? I can't see Madame Arcana any more. There's no sign of Fitzroy and the chap that said he's gone off to find more information on these people has, well, gone off.'

'But he will have at least told the police and others to cooperate with us,' I said. 'It would be insane not to.'

'I do not think the chap - blast it, why could he not give us a name? I will call him Michael. I do not think Michael knows much beyond his limited scope. After all, there was that talk about compartmentalised knowledge, was there not?'

'You mean when Madame Arcana said they did not know much about each other? That Fitzroy was essentially the linchpin.'

'Aye, I can see him loving that,' said Rory darkly.

'So, we will need to introduce ourselves as servants of the crown?' I said.

'Exactly,' said Bertram. 'Except we do not all need to do so, do we?'

Rory and I exchanged glances. 'The German delegation - and the Brits for that matter, will be able to work out that Euphemia and I work together because of our escapades earlier, but they do not know McLeod.'

Rory frowned. 'Are you saying I do not have the right credentials? Fitzroy asked for me as much as you.'

'You misunderstand,' said Bertram. 'I am saying this is a good thing. Euphemia and I have worked alone before. If we can convince them to let you through the cordon again - say you are my servant or chauffeur...'

'Or some other person of low importance,' growled

Rory.

'Oh, I see,' I said. 'How clever, Bertram. Rory can go back and see if there are leads we haven't explored at the hotel.'

'You want me to find the twins,' said Rory, raising his eyebrows.

'Look,' said Bertram, 'I know I must serve my country, but I am damned if I am going to turn my back on my own sister and her children. I might not be able to scour for leads, but I can send the man I trust the most to do so.'

'I know I said I thought that when one piece of the puzzle was solved the others would reveal themselves, and that may well still be true,' I said, 'But I would be happier if one of us could interview the hotel staff and be there to support Richenda.'

'I'm honoured you would trust me,' said Rory gruffly. He got to his feet. 'I'll get through that cordon if I have to fight my way through.'

Fortunately, this proved to be unnecessary. We despatched Rory back to the hotel and introduced ourselves to the police doctor, a Dr P.K. Cambridge. His name was printed in neat gold lettering along his doctor's bag and his suit was well cut and pressed. He had a perfectly trimmed beard, and hands with such astonishingly long and elegant fingers they drew your attention almost as much as his light grey eyes did. He moved with grace about the fallen Von Ritter, but at the same time there was a suppressed energy that hinted that any moment he might sprint into the distance. A man more alive I have rarely seen and yet he had chosen to work with the dead.

'Dr Cambridge,' I said. 'We are with the Crown and have been asked to investigate this matter.'

He looked up from his kneeling position beside the corpse. 'Not overcome with hysterics by being so close to a dead body, young lady? He is dead, you know. As dead as a body that has been in the ground a fortnight.'

'But not yet consumed by maggots,' I said tartly. 'I presume you are not suggesting that the Baron was a wandering corpse. We believe his death occurred within the hour.'

Dr Cambridge gave out a crack of laughter. 'They are who they claim to be, George,' he called over to a worried-looking police officer. 'Only one of their females could be so callous.' I heard Bertram move behind me as if to defend me. I stepped back casually onto this foot. Poor Bertram, I thought, I used this tactic so often I should consider buying him some reinforced shoes for a wedding present.

'But, yes, that's what the other fellows tell us,' said Dr Cambridge to me. 'There's no better way I know of assessing time more accurately than rigor and I am one of the best cutters around.'

'What caused his death?' asked Bertram from behind me.

'He's dead because his heart is no longer working,' said the doctor.

'What caused it to stop beating?' I asked.

The doctor stood up. He towered over both Bertram and I, but being of slender frame he did not loom. He brushed his hands together as if ridding them of the stench of death. 'Well, that's the question, is it not, or you lot would not be here, hmm?'

'Doctor, if you could answer the question to the best of your ability,' I said coldly. I stepped back, so I could look him in the eye. Bertram dodged and came up on my right side.

'I presume you do not require a theory on the metaphysical aspects of when a man's time is nigh?'

'Hardly,' said Bertram drily.

'It appears to have been a heart attack,' said the doctor. At this point, if he had been smaller I might well have seriously considered slapping his face.

'We have already been told this,' I said.

'I expect you have also been told of Dr Gardener mentioning he smelled almonds, and what that might mean. Seems a good man, Gardener. I am confident if there was anything to be done, he did it. No, the old Hun here dropped like a stone.'

'Speculate,' I said. I had no idea why everyone was going on about almonds. They might have been referring to an allergy, but I did not wish to display my ignorance.

'Oh no, you simply will not get me that way. His death certificate will say he died of heart failure. What caused that is beyond my ability to say. There may have been a slight foaming at the mouth. Yes, that could be a result of poisoning, but he could also be one of those types who have overactive saliva glands. You know, the ones that one generally finds oneself sitting next to in theatres. Gulpers.'

'You do not appear to be taking this situation seriously,' said Bertram.

'I can assure you I am taking it very seriously,' said Cambridge. 'I am being very careful not to say or suggest anything that cannot be irrevocably proved in a court of law. When I get him up on the table it is possible I might find something else. Like a blood clot somewhere. But there is nothing more I can say just by viewing him from the outside. If you will let me get away, I shall get him up on the slab as a priority and have a good rummage.'

148

'Let him go,' said Bertram to me.

I nodded and stepped away. The police officer who had responded to being called George, a youngish man with blond hair and a very pale complexion, came over to me. He wore a heavily trimmed cap and had epaulettes that suggested rank, but whose significance was unknown to me. 'He is a fine doctor, Cambridge,' he said. 'We use him for all the difficult cases. He is very precise in his reports. What he says always holds up.' He coloured very slightly. 'We tend to overlook his - err - quirky mannerisms.'

'We have a list of people we would like to interview,' said Bertram.

'I drew it up,' said the officer. 'I have people waiting for you in as separate an area of the exhibition as I could arrange.'

'Have you taken statements from members of the public, any who were close enough to witness the group before, during and after the event?' I asked.

The officer nodded. 'It is all waiting for you, but I have to say, at first sight, it does not look promising from the informative aspect of the situation. To all intents and purposes, it appears that the gentleman died an unfortunate, but natural death.'

'So why are the public being kept here?' I asked. 'Surely it would be easier to let them go?'

'I agree, ma'am,' said the officer, 'But the German members of the delegation believe this to be murder and are unwilling to let anyone leave until all the names and addresses have been collected. Even then I think it likely they will ask they remain until the investigation is resolved.'

'If they are waiting on German officers to appear,' said Bertram, 'that could take days. How ridiculous!'

149

'I believe they are hoping officials from their embassy will shortly arrive.'

'What nonsense,' I said. 'They already have senior members of the diplomatic staff here. If they are waiting on more specialist staff I would imagine His Majesty would not be at all happy about them operating in what remains an area of the British Empire. No one has done something stupid and declared Crystal Palace neutral ground or German sovereign ground for the exhibition, have they?'

'Not that I know of,' said the officer. 'Could it be done?'

'Not, I believe, without making it an embassy,' I said. 'So, officer, if you believe you have gathered what you can from members of the public and no longer require their presence, I suggest they are no longer detained from going about their rightful business. They are citizens of the British Empire and not Germany,' I said stoutly.

'Thank you, ma'am,' said the officer. 'I only needed someone to say the word. We have a lot of unhappy people. They are hot, tired and some of the ladies have been threatening to faint.'

'In that case you must certainly release them,' I said.

'And Dr Gardener?'

'As soon as you can verify that he is Dr Gardener, and does reside at the address he has given, he may also depart. He has given us a written statement I take it? I do not think his attempt at helping the dying man should be rewarded with restraint.'

'That makes sense,' said the officer. 'I will release him as soon as we can confirm his identity. I should have thought of that myself.'

'This is hardly an everyday occurrence,' I said kindly.

'I think you and your men have done a remarkable job. If you could show my colleague and I to the interview room, we can move things along.'

'The other members of the delegation?'

'It goes without saying they cannot leave the country until this mystery is solved,' said Bertram. 'But from what you have said it does not sound like they want to go anyway. See if you can corral them back at their hotel, will you? Unless of course it is the Carlton. It is not, is it?' said Bertram.

'No,' said the officer.

'Excellent,' said Bertram. 'Then lead on. Perhaps there is somewhere we could confer before we see the first suspect?'

Officer George led us away to a small office that the manager of the Palace used. As soon as we were alone Bertram said, 'Gosh, Euphemia, you were rather magnificent. I do hope Fitzroy will not mind that we have been ordering the police about.'

'If he minded about such things he should be here,' I snapped. 'Goodness, Bertram. I do not know if I did the right thing or not, but it seemed to me we had to assert our authority, not simply over the police but over the men we are to question. If a German national has been murdered on British soil it is no time for us to show weakness.'

Bertram muttered something which sounded rather like a repeat of 'magnificent', but I chose not to hear. 'Do we think he was murdered?' I said. 'And why does everyone keep going on about almonds?'

'I thought at first they meant Germans always smelled like that. They do like those marzipan cakes. But, on thinking it over, I think it must have some connection to a kind of quick-acting poison. Cambridge seemed to know what it meant, and I got the distinct impression from him he would not comment on it because he did not expect to find any medical evidence one way or another.'

'That was my thought too.'

'About the cakes?'

'No, about Cambridge not being willing to provide any possibilities. I have also been thinking about the list "Michael" gave us. Other than Von Ritter's aide, if it is murder, we are left with a fifty-fifty chance of it being a German or a British citizen. It is not a comfortable position to be in.'

'What? No,' said Bertram. 'It is a stuffy little office.'

I sighed inwardly and let him finish his thought. The vaguer Bertram becomes, the more useful the information he processes often is. Of course, there are also times when it merely means he is hungry.

'Nasty little thought I am having,' he said at last. 'You do not think Fitzroy has gone missing because this murder is one of his operations? I mean, he says he is on the anti-war side, but is anything that man says ever to be taken as truth.'

'That would mean he has put us in a dire position because either he expects us to cover for him,' I said.

'Or he thinks we are not bright enough to figure it out,' said Bertram.

'He's a fool if he thinks that,' I said.

Bertram smiled at me. 'Who shall we start with? And what shall we ask?'

'We know so very little,' I said, 'I think we had better appear to know a lot.'

Bertram blinked at me. 'You mean if we keep schtum they might blurt out the truth?'

'I do not expect a confession. We don't even know if

these men have families and have only the vaguest notion of their occupations. If we let them see how little we have, they will not take us seriously. So, yes, I think we ask them to relay what they saw and then ask if they wish to add anything further.'

'Should we try and look menacing?' said Bertram, looking anxious.

Despite the dire circumstances this day had wrought upon us, I was of half a mind to ask Bertram to show me his menacing look, but I decided not to tease him. 'I am not sure what manner we should adopt. We cannot seem suspicious, anxious, jovial, afraid or aggressive. What does that leave?'

'Professional?' suggested Bertram.

'I suppose,' I said. 'It would make a change from the manner Fitzroy generally adopts.'

Bertram raised an eyebrow.

'I suppose you would call it casual callousness?' I said. 'With a touch of very dry humour.'

'Hmm. I definitely cannot do that, and as a gentleman it goes against the grain to appear as if I am from a profession, but I will do my best.'

I stilled the twitching of my lips. 'It is the most anyone could ask,' I said.

Our first interviewee was Friedrich Gottlieb. We found him sitting slumped at a small table his head in his hands. We sat down quietly opposite him. He looked up and assumed an expression of loathing.

'You!' said Gottlieb. 'I knew all that fainting was a pretence. Your appearance at the séance was no coincidence either. You were manipulating the Baron and when your obvious ploys did not change his mind, you killed him. You British are dogs.'

153

'Always rather liked dogs,' said Bertram. Gottlieb looked suitably surprised that Bertram did not rise to the bait. I was impressed.

'Your opinion on our movements is irrelevant,' I said. 'Can you explain your position next to Von Ritter when he died and your subsequent actions.'

'I am his aide. I translated the more awkward words and ensured he had all he needed. He had expressed a desire for a cup of tea. I fetched it for him from the tea shop. He took no more than two sips before he was taken ill. He collapsed. I called for a doctor and loosened his collar. I reassured him help was on its way. A British doctor came to our aid, but he appeared unable to help and the Baron died.'

'I say, I do not like your tone.' said Bertram. 'I am certain the man did his best.'

'It is possible that British doctors are not as good as German ones,' sneered Gottlieb.

'So, you were the last one to give Von Ritter anything he ate or drank?' I said. 'Will the others confirm that.'

Gottlieb paled slightly at that. 'There were witnesses, both German and English, who will tell you as much.'

'Did anyone else handle the cup?' said Bertram.

'The woman who poured it,' said Gottlieb with obvious sarcasm. 'A *grosse* Frau.' Bertram blushed.

'The lady has already been identified,' I said. 'I believe you asked for tea and did not mention it was for the Baron?'

Bertram glanced askance at me, but I ignored him. 'That is true,' said Gottlieb. 'But it would be not unreasonable to assume that if I were to fetch a tea for myself then I would also do so for the Baron and I was known to be his aide.'

'Did the Baron have a fondness for English tea?' I asked.

'No,' said Gottlieb. 'He abhorred it, as he did your cuisine.'

I waited and let that sink in.

'You think someone was trying to kill *me*?' said Gottlieb. 'I am no one.'

'Firstly, we have yet to establish that the Baron's death was anything more than a natural, but tragic, act of nature, and secondly that if this was murder that it had anything to do with the tea. Did he also partake of any cake? Perhaps a marzipan one? I believe German people are fond of marzipan.'

Gottlieb narrowed his eyes. 'What are you telling me?' he said.

'I am the one asking questions.'

'But you ask about a particular cake for a reason, I think?' His accent became more German with this question. I knew I was missing something, but it also appeared I had him on the back foot. I decided to push a little harder.

'I believe you were a last-minute replacement for the Baron's aide and that you do not generally move in diplomatic circles.'

Gottlieb's outline softened slightly. Damn! I had asked the wrong question. 'It is no mystery. His diplomatic aide became unable to attend, at the last moment. The Baron did not wish someone he did not know to accompany him on this mission. I am a senior shipping clerk at his company and have frequently acted as his personal secretary. He felt he could trust me.'

Fitzroy would think such a placement good cover for a spy. 'How convenient you were free,' I said.

'Yes, was it not?' said Gottlieb with a thin-lipped smile.

'That will be all for now,' I said. 'The attendants will do their best to make you comfortable until you can be sent back to your hotel.'

'Intolerable,' said Gottlieb, but he rose quickly enough and exited the room. When the door closed behind him, Bertram spoke, the words bursting out of him.

'The man is a spy!' he said.

'It would seem so,' I said.

'You do not seem very alarmed.'

'Fitzroy is a spy. Michael is a spy. We might even be considered acting as spies.'

'But he is one of *theirs*,' said Bertram. 'He's a Hun! On British soil!'

'He is a man doing his job,' I said.

'Euphemia!'

'I am certain Fitzroy has more than once been on German soil and I would not be surprised if he had, as he might put it, "removed a person who had become a threat to the crown".' Bertram opened his mouth. I held up my hand to forestall him. 'I do not say I approve of these actions. But I will not be a hypocrite either. Gottlieb is likely as loyal to his Kaiser as Fitzroy is to his King.'

'You have spent altogether far too much time with Fitzroy,' said Bertram. 'His influence over you has become shockingly strong. When we are married…'

I interrupted with an icy, 'Yes?'

Bertram sighed. 'When we are married you will carry on doing exactly as you please.'

'But I will seek and consider your opinion,' I said. Bertram gave me a doleful look.

Our next interviewee was Rudolf Beiersdorf. It took

only a few minutes to ascertain that he and the Baron had been good friends for a long time. The man was deeply affected and on the verge of tears. I estimated him to be around the same age as Klaus Von Ritter, but while Von Ritter had adopted the latest fashions and made an effort to look dashing, Beiersdorf was more like a Germanic Santa Claus. I felt more inclined to fetch him a whisky and a comfy cushion than I did to question him. Bertram did most of the enquiry. I determined to study if his emotions were true, and they did appear to me so; unless he was the most consummate actor. I tuned in to hear him saying, 'Of course, Klaus was no angel. His wife, Marie - has she been wired? The poor soul. She doted on him. Two sons and four daughters they have. She had a lot of trouble with him at the beginning, but in the end, she accepted him for the way he was. Klaus gave her affection, children, a grand home and all the trinkets she could wish for. Her life was better than many women of her station. So what if he had the occasional fancy. He was her husband. The poor, poor, woman. I do not know how she will cope.'

Bertram let him go shortly after that. After he left he took out his handkerchief and patted at the sweat on his forehead. 'Is this getting too much?' I asked. 'Are you in pain? We can take a respite.' Bertram's 'dicky heart', as he terms it, is the bane of our lives. I live in fear that one argument too many, one escapade too many, will tear him from my side for ever. But for all that I know he does not want a submissive wife or a quiet life. Perhaps it is because of his poor health that it is important to him to feel alive, to throw himself into one daft adventure after another – even to fall in love with me. A woman who, as far as he knows, is no more than a maid risen above her station in the world.

Bertram gave me an odd look; almost as if he could read my thoughts. But before we could discuss the matter further Algernon Porter stormed into the room. He had a full head of bushy white hair and startling mutton-chops. 'Where the hell is Fitzroy?' he demanded.

'A question which is also vexing us,' I said calmly, indicating he should take a seat.

'If you think I am going to be interviewed like some criminal by some jumped-up amateurs you can damn well think again.'

'Of course not,' I said soothingly. 'But it is important that the German delegation believe we are questioning all the people around Von Ritter in the same manner and showing no preference. I believe he had been pro-war, but was changing his mind?'

'Yes, ruddy shame. He's behind many of the German Navy boats from what we can gather. Him being against the war would have been a coup. Has the ear of the Kaiser I believe.'

'So, you think war can be averted?' said Bertram.

'Hell's teeth,' said Porter. 'Don't you lot know anything! Of course it bloody can't. But if we can at least defer it a little longer we can get more of our dreadnoughts into position.'

I took a bold stroke. 'I understand His Majesty is against the war.'

Porter fussed with his collar and tie. 'Of course. Of course. Rather all too in the family for him. He would rather it did not happen. Does not want to endanger the lives of citizens of the British Empire, but sometimes blood has to be spilled to prevent greater bloodshed, don'tcha know?'

I did not know any such thing, but I was getting the

measure of Porter and I did not much like it.

'Do you think anyone in the delegation might have wished Von Ritter harm?' said Bertram.

Porter frowned, looking rather like an irate Father Time. 'He seemed to get on well enough with Beiersdorf and the lad, whom he'd known since he was knee-high to a grasshopper by all accounts. It goes without saying no one on our side is under suspicion.' He glared at me from under his eyebrows. I gave him a polite non-committal smile.

'Perhaps we might consider who he had been in contact with over the past few days?' I said. 'Other than the Exhibition, where has the delegation been?'

'We did a brief tour of the Royal Mint,' said Porter. 'Drove them round some of the sites. Waterloo House and all that. Showed them Westminster from the outside. It was thought too formal to take them inside. Besides, can't control damned politicians. Never know what the buggers are going to say or do next. Could have thrown a bucket load of spanners in the works, don'tcha know? Of course, we took them all to my club, but the less said about that the better.'

'What do you mean?' said Bertram.

'My club is Bosenby's,' said Porter. He coughed. 'Family tradition.'

'Bosenby's?' I said.

'Gentlemen only,' said Porter. 'Can't discuss with a lady, don'tcha know?'

Dietrich Habermann, the German diplomat, could not have been a stronger counterpoint to Porter. He was exquisitely polite and the first man to pull out my chair and insist I sat first. Blond, blue-eyed, tall and well-formed, he was a walking advertisement for Germany. I

159

could tell Bertram, who is a little on the short side, disliked him at first sight. But even he had to admit Habermann spoke openly and with candour.

'Baron Von Ritter is… was a popular gentleman. He has a large family, a devoted wife and a thriving business. I would not say he was often at the Kaiser's side, but he was known to have the Kaiser's trust. It is very much the case that Von Ritter stayed away from politics unless he felt he had something important and urgent to say. As a nobleman he was rather refreshing, although I believe his background might not hold up to a herald's scrutiny. This may explain why he was always so reasonable.' He gave a wry smile. 'He had his faults, but he was discreet. He was also a little too fond of wine, cigars and good eating. It is sad, but not a surprise that his heart gave out. I assume this enquiry is merely to show that all that could be done was done.'

'We also have to rule out any foul play,' I said.

'Very honest of you to own up to that,' said Habermann. 'It is difficult to see why one might dislike Klaus enough to kill him. Yes, it is known he had been pro-war, but he was softening. In other words, he was still there to be persuaded by either side. In my position at the embassy I can assure you that he sent no directions home that would indicate he had fastened to one position. Of course, you have only my word on that, but German gentlemen hold their honour as dear as Englishmen do.'

I nodded. 'What you are saying is that both factions for and against war on both sides had all to play for with Baron Von Ritter.'

'A delightful expression, "all to play for", but yes, indeed, it sums up the situation nicely.'

'Was there any rivalry between him and Mr Draper - or

even Herr Beiersdorf?' Bertram asked.

'I am not aware of any,' said Habermann. 'I do my best to keep abreast of such things – as I am sure do your department. As far as I knew Beiersdorf and Von Ritter were old friends. Von Ritter and Draper will have met in business circles, but I am unaware of any direct links or social involvement. During the meetings of the delegation they appeared civil enough to each other. Draper is younger and, if you will forgive me, of a different class. I believe they had little in common.'

'Do you know of anyone who might have reason to harm the Baron?' I said.

'You mean his aide?' said Habermann. 'They argued more than I would have imagined a man of his position would allow. Although, if I am scrupulously fair, Gottlieb was never rude when expressing a differing position. I am, of course, aware he gave Von Ritter the tea after which he became ill, but I do not believe he had any motive to murder Von Ritter. If anything, I believe the Baron thought of him fondly. He was an indulgent and philanthropic employer. His reputation stands to that.'

'And the rest of his reputation?' asked Bertram quietly.

Habermann darted a glance in my direction. 'I see. You have heard he had a certain peccadillo. That is true. For a man his age he was, in some ways,' again he looked at me, 'spry. However, he was wealthy enough that I do not believe there was ever - how could one say? A badness left behind.'

'Bad feelings?' said Bertram.

'Exactly,' said Habermann. 'He behaved like a gentleman. Or, as I believe, a gentleman should.' Bertram raised his eyebrows at this but did not respond verbally.

This left us with only the British magnate of industry,

Robert Draper, a self-made man who was still only in his mid-thirties. He wore an excellent suit, but his nails were unmanicured and his hair in need of a decent cut. Despite this, he was clean-shaven.

'Do you think someone offed the Hun?' he said, sitting down without invitation. 'I'll tell you now, I am a plain man, who speaks plain. Klaus Von Ritter and I were not friends, but neither were we enemies. He had the ways of a toff, even though I believe he came up through the ranks like I did. Married into the German aristocracy and got them all eating out of his hand with his charm, but I saw through that.'

'Did you, Mr Draper. What did you see?' I asked.

'I saw a wary man, who kept his cards close to his chest and knew how to make friends in the right places. Every move he made was calculated. This whole, do I or don't I want to go to war? Why, that was all over contracts. He'd have gone whichever way the money did. Any businessman would.'

'As you will?' I asked.

'I can see you think the less of me for that, but I am no different from the others. I merely say what they hide. I am as loyal a subject of King and Country as any man. If His Majesty directs me this way or that I will follow without hesitation, but while he is still making his mind up, I will go where the money is.'

Bertram sighed. It was a position he was all too familiar with from his own family. 'In summary, Von Ritter was nothing to you, so you had no reason to harm him?'

'More likely to be the other way around. I knew him for what he was. I saw through his act.'

'Did you challenge him on it?' I asked. 'This act you saw.'

'No, why would I?' said Draper. 'Each man makes his way the best he can in the world according to his God and his conscience.'

'Did you see anything untoward on the day or even during the trip?' asked Bertram.

'In what way?' said Draper. 'Everyone was being very polite to one another. Typically, I retired first. There is only so much falseness I can take.' He looked at me. 'You of all people should get that, love, considering your occupation. That lot are carrying on as if they are all best friends, but the word comes down from the Royal courts that we're to fight and tomorrow we could be shooting each other on the battlefield. If you think anyone is going to make friends with someone who they might be looking at from the wrong end of a gun barrel shortly, you can think again.'

'Some might think that sensible - to make friends, I mean,' I said.

'Aye,' said Draper. 'And others might call it treason. I have a mind to stay out of the politics. I will go back to my steel mills and we will keep rolling. There is never any shortage of buyers. War or no war, that will remain the same.'

'Today,' said Bertram, 'when he was given a cup of tea, did you see anyone near it?'

'His aide, that Gottlieb, fetched it. The old man was looking a bit green around the gills. No surprise, despite the "wonders of the palace's ventilation system".' He spoke these last words mockingly. 'It was pretty warm for an older gent who's carrying a lifetime of excellent dinners around with him. Not that I think he wanted tea, but that was all that was on offer. Let me think. He looked pale and asked to sit. Porter diverted us to the tea room. Beiersdorf hung around Von Ritter, fussing like an old woman. Habermann did the sensible thing and went off to see if a doctor could be found. He brought back Dr Gardener, but it was all too late by then. I think Porter made some fuss about fresh water being used for the tea. Likes to make his presence felt, that one. Nothing new in that. Less sense than a cat, that man. If we were all looking at a fire, damn me, that man would go and sit in the middle of it.'

'You have been very helpful,' said Bertram. 'Thank you, Mr Draper.'

Chapter Twelve
Picking a Scape-goat

I sat down with my notebook and considered our options. 'It is still cloudy to me,' I said. 'It seems we can rule out Herr Habermann.'

'I agree,' said Bertram. 'Quite glad of that. The only one of 'em who struck me as a gentleman.'

'I felt Herr Beiersdorf was genuinely distraught at Von Ritter's death, but I do not feel I can rule out that he might have felt duty bound to kill him over something or other?'

'You mean the word of the Kaiser? A bit far-fetched, Euphemia. The man is like Father Christmas.'

I smiled broadly. 'That is exactly how he struck me. I do not think we have evidence to totally rule him out, but I do not expect him to be a murderer.'

Bertram nodded. 'I see what you mean. Long odds, but still in the race. I say, we do still think the chap was murdered, don't we?'

'I was hoping Dr Cambridge would have got back to us with some information by now.' I hesitated. 'The thing is, if it did turn out to be a British member of the delegation, I do not think Fitzroy would wish us to disclose that to the Germans. He would rather we went with a heart attack as being the cause of death.'

'Then why are we doing all this?' said Bertram crossly.

'Because whatever action Fitzroy may decide upon he will want to know the truth. I can understand why we might not wish the Germans to know one of their nationals was killed on our soil by one of our citizens. Goodness, I imagine wars have started over far less.'

'I see your point,' said Bertram grimly.

'However, I would certainly urge for any British person to be prosecuted to the full extent of the law - or at the very least brought to justice for their action - but not necessarily publicly.'

'Damn it, Euphemia! This is just the kind of nonsense we swore we would not get involved with again. Private justice is but one step away from a dictatorship! I cannot believe the King condones any such action.'

'Do we then let the murderer go free if he is British?' I countered. 'Let us suppose this murder was merely for self-gain and not national interest - because I do not think Fitzroy or his people would condone this investigation if there was a hint of political assignation. I have dwelt on this. Amateurs though we are - assets even - we have a reputation for unearthing the truth.'

Bertram nodded. 'We are a good team. But you were saying if this is a common murder, what then?'

'Then we cannot allow the actions of one man and the life of another to endanger millions of others. If war remains in the wings we must step lightly. We must investigate to the Germans' satisfaction, but should the murderer prove to be British we must conceal it from them.'

'You do not think they would trust us all the more if we handed the murderer over to them?' said Bertram.

'I have neither the knowledge nor the experience to make that decision,' I said.

'Where is ruddy Fitzroy!' said Bertram. He stood and began to pace. He paused after a couple of turns. 'By the way, Euphemia, I am dreadfully sorry you're mixed up in this business. It's nothing to do with us and it seems particularly nasty this time.'

'Thank you, Bertram. Normally I would assure you I am the equal to anything, but this time I understand your desire to protect me. Having the fate of the peoples of two countries in our hands is a heavy and unwelcome burden,' I said, a warm feeling blossoming in my chest that Bertram wished to shield me from the realities of the world. There was a time when I would have been angry at such intentions, but now I had seen the world for what it was, I quite fancied protection from it. I would, naturally, do the same for him.

'To get back to the suspects: Gottlieb has to be a prime one. We know Fitzroy suspected him for turning up at the last minute. Gottlieb didn't even mention that the man whose place he took had died. I find that most suspicious.'

'He might have thought that's what we would think - drat it! You know what I mean. Besides, do you not think there was some truth in Von Ritter wanting an aide he knew?'

'Perhaps,' I admitted. 'But they did argue.'

'And he indulged him,' said Bertram. 'I have a theory about that. But go on.'

'I find Porter repulsive, but I cannot see him endangering his career, nor any reason for him to harm Von Ritter.'

'We know Porter likes to be the centre of attention,' said Bertram. 'There may be something in that.'

'Robert Draper obviously considers himself refreshingly honest,' I said. 'I found him common and repugnant, but he is the one who gave us the clearest picture of what occurred.'

'You think he is telling the truth?' asked Bertram.

I nodded. 'He knows we can verify everything he says,

not only with the others in the delegation, but with the statements the police have taken. In fact, we should do that now. Those at a distance will have seen best.'

Bertram heaved a huge sigh and turned to the pile of papers the police had left us. 'Do you think we could get them to bring us some tea?'

'You really want tea from that tea shop?' I asked.

'Hell's bells!' said Bertram. 'Sorry, Euphemia, but do we actually consider the tea lady?'

'I think we get Michael to do a background check on her,' I said. 'But she could not have been certain the tea was for Von Ritter nor that he would even want tea. I think she is most unlikely.'

'Good,' said Bertram. 'We have enough suspects.' He picked up the papers and split them with me. 'I wonder how Rory is getting on?'

'The sooner we get through this lot, the sooner we will able to find out,' I said and bent my head over the first statement.

The police had been thorough. We were able to substantiate Draper's description of the scene. All the witnesses also placed Draper at a table away from the others, where he had been enjoying a solitary cake during the unplanned break. A waiter further confirmed that Draper had been so argumentative with Porter over luncheon that much of his meal had gone uneaten. The exact nature of the disagreement was unclear. Michael had yet to return, but it was becoming clear that we had not moved much further forward. We had ruled out Habermann. Draper appeared to have been too far away. We thought Beiersdorf unlikely. We agreed our favoured suspect was Gottlieb, the aide, but we had no adequate motive. Algernon Porter could not be dismissed, but we again had no good reason to include him. At least we knew that Gottlieb and Von Klaus had argued.

'That makes him my first choice,' I said.

'First choice to be hanged,' said Bertram. 'We cannot get this wrong.'

'I hope Cambridge comes up with some perfect proof of natural death.'

'If he had found one I think he would have been in contact by now. We know Von Ritter had a heart attack. We do not know if it was chemically induced,' said Bertram.

'Will we ever know?' I said.

'Without a confession,' said Bertram. 'It is does not look good.'

I banged my hand on the table so hard it hurt. 'Damn all this! I want to get back to Rory and Richenda.'

'We could say that we believe this was nothing but a heart attack,' said Bertram. 'That may well turn out to be our conclusion anyway. The evidence is not thick on the ground. We could save time and go for that option now.'

I looked over at him. There were more lines on his face than when we had first met. He was frowning.

'We cannot,' I said and I saw the frown lift.

'I know it is hard not being able to rush to Richenda's side,' said Bertram. 'But I do not think you could live with yourself if you did not do your best to establish the truth here.'

I smiled. 'Neither could you,' I said.

He smiled sadly back at me. 'Then let's hope we can uncover the truth and that you were right, this mystery is linked to the twins' disappearance.' At this moment Michael chose to make his entrance.

Michael's collar stood proud, but only that. His clothes

hung off him in creases. Shadows ringed his eyes. A great purple bruise was blooming across this cheek.

'What the hell happened to you?' said Bertram.

'The situation was not straightforward,' said Michael laconically, slumping into a chair. 'Do you have a culprit.'

'What is the importance of almonds?' said Bertram.

'It can be an indication of a fast-acting poison,' said Michael. 'I thought you would know that.'

'Why would we know that?' I snapped. 'As Fitzroy has often been at pains to point out, we are assets, not operatives.'

'Are you not up to the task?'

'We have ruled out Habermann and Draper. Beiersdorf is a low probability,' I said. 'Gottlieb appears the prime suspect, but we have no motive. We are hoping you can supply one. Fitzroy suspected him of being a foreign operative.'

'I cannot confirm that,' said Michael. 'I can, however, tell you there is a strong rumour that Gottlieb was Von Ritter's illegitimate son.'

'Bosenby's,' said Bertram.

'What about it?' said Michael.

'It's Porter's club. He said he took Von Klaus there.'

Michael nodded. 'It fits with the profile I have been building.'

'Could you kindly explain what is so special about this club?' I said. The men exchanged looks. 'If you intend to treat me as an equal, and I strongly suggest you do, Michael, you will give me this information.'

'Michael?'

Bertram coughed. 'We didn't know your name, so we gave you one. Easier that referring to "that man", et cetera.'

'Fair enough,' said Michael, not bothering to inform us of his actual name. He looked at me. 'Fitzroy is always so careful about you,' he said enigmatically. 'I cannot work out your relationship.'

I bridled at that. 'I am engaged to Bertram,' I said.

'How does that make any difference?' said Michael. He paused. 'Bosenby's has a certain reputation. It allows women on the premises, but only of a certain kind.'

'You are suggesting Von Ritter was a philanderer,' I said. 'It fits with how he treated me - and I could have told you that if you had both not been so coy earlier.'

Bertram started to splutter into anger. Michael interrupted him. 'The man's dead, so that is moot. I am uncomfortable with the way in which you have not ruled out some of the others definitively. Is there anything from Cambridge?'

'Not yet,' said Bertram.

'The information I have for you is little and hard-won. Beiersdorf is a long-standing friend of Von Ritter, but he was engaged to Ritter's wife, before she chose to marry the Baron. The Baron is known to have made his wife extremely unhappy in the early days, and his philandering has continued, though to a lesser degree, into his later years. Apparently, his wife is pregnant yet again and the doctors are concerned for her life. It would be a long time to hold a grudge, but the woman's impending possible demise might have rekindled it.'

'Poisoning on foreign soil makes him less likely to be suspected,' I said. 'But it sounds as if he would require a degree of forward planning. Could a man wait for revenge for so long?'

Michael shrugged. 'I could. Anyway, Draper is not well liked by those in power. He is expecting a knighthood for his support should there be a war. He is liable to get one too. We need him. However, he has strong anti-establishment leanings and has been suspected of Bolshevik sympathies.' Bertram groaned at this.

'Porter is rising fast. Liable to cross the line into politics shortly and tipped for greatness. I cannot discover any link to Von Ritter nor why he would risk such an action at this time. Habermann is more of a dark horse. Stainless character. Excellent diplomat. Scrupulously clean private life. Highly suspicious.'

'We did wonder about the tea lady,' said Bertram.

'Oh, they're all ours. You would hardly believe the types we enrol as assets.' His tone made me uncomfortable.

'So you are suspicious of Habermann,' I said, attempting to redirect the conversation.

'Very,' said Michael.

'Oh, did we mention that Gottlieb had been heard arguing with Von Ritter. Can't recall who told us,' said Bertram. 'But it should be easy to check.'

'Publicly?' said Michael.

'It was certainly overheard,' I answered.

'I suppose that wraps it up,' said Michael, in a stunning about-face. 'All that needs to be decided is if we hang him here or hand him over to Germany.'

'But he'll go to trial,' said Bertram.

'Hmm, unlikely,' said Michael. 'Be awkward at this stage. As long as the Germans see we have acted in a just and unbiased manner, it should be all right. I'm thinking we hand him over to them and let them sort it out. Publicly we call it a heart attack. We can say we were taking security precautions that proved unnecessary. That should go down well both here and abroad.' He stood up. 'Your country thanks you for your service.'

'Wait a minute,' I said. 'Is that it? You are sentencing Gottlieb to death just like that? A minute ago you were prepared to hand over Habermann as the murderer.'

'I am not the one who found the evidence,' said Michael. He sighed. 'This is what happens when you involve civilians too deeply. If I have told Fitzroy once I have told him a hundred times...'

'Is he back?' asked Bertram.

Michael shook his head. He looked at me. 'What do you want?'

'For the man to get a fair trial!'

'He is not a British citizen. If we hand him back to the Germans with our suspicions it is out of our hands.'

'What do you think will happen to him?' asked Bertram.

Michael shrugged. 'Probably best for all if he falls off the boat on the way home.'

'This is not right!' I protested.

'We - or rather you - could argue around this for hours. What did you think you were doing? We need a name. You gave us one.'

'Give us more time to ensure it is the right one,' I said.

Michael frowned. 'This needs to be wrapped up quickly.'

'And we have other things to do,' said Bertram. 'Urgent things.'

'We cannot risk sending an innocent man to his death,' I said.

'Look,' said Michael, 'you are devout Christians. Think of it as him simply getting to the promised land earlier. All I want is someone we can reasonably suggest is the murderer. I don't care who it is. What's that saying about

173

letting God sort the sinners from the righteous?'

The look of loathing I gave him at such blasphemy made him wince slightly.

'All right. You have until tomorrow morning. Then a name must be given and whomever that is will face terminal consequences. You understand that attributing this murder is to placate the peace process – to keep it alive. The death of one innocent man for the potential deaths of thousands of innocent men. It is the kind of deal this country and its rulers must make every day.'

'But you said there will be war anyway,' I said.

'I am not omniscient,' said Michael. 'There is always a chance peace might prove more profitable.' He pushed in his chair with an air of finality. 'You have until tomorrow morning at eight a.m. That is when the delegation will be sitting down together again for breakfast. I will lift the cordon now and send them back to their hotel. Escorts will ensure none of them mingle or leave.' Then he left.

Bertram regarded me with a mixture of admiration and despair. 'I do not know whether to applaud you for your conscientiousness or despair that this keeps us longer from helping Richenda.' He stood and came over to me. He took one of my hands in both of his and looked me directly in the eyes. 'What do you think we can achieve now? It sounded very much to me as if Michael has put the delegation out of our reach. The day is drawing to a close. The twins and Merry are still missing. The exhibition is closing. What can we actually do with this extra time?'

'Bosenby's,' I said. 'We can talk to the staff and any witnesses we can find about last night. A picture of how the group behaved socially may give us a fresh insight. If it does, we can return to their hotel at seven a.m. and demand to re-question the group based on our new evidence.'

'No,' said Bertram.

'No? No to what?'

'You cannot go to Bosenby's. If you insist I will go and discover what I can, but you cannot accompany me. Do not ask,' said Bertram.

'I have no intention of asking,' I said. 'We should return to our hotel, so we can change.'

Bertram scowled. 'It is not like you to capitulate so easily,' he said.

'Come,' I said. 'It may be that Rory has news about the babies.'

Bertram took my arm and we walked unimpeded to the cab rank. He said nothing more but appeared to have developed a mild tic. He kept glancing at me out of the corner of his eye. I, as usual, concentrated on keeping us on a straight course.

Chapter Thirteen
A Situation So Fraught Not Even Cake Will Help

At the hotel suite Rory flung open the door to our knock. Shirt sleeves rolled up to his elbows and sporting grazed and bleeding knuckles, his appearance drew a gasp of astonishment from both of us.

'I found someone,' he said, panting slightly. 'He has not told me everything yet, but he will.'

I pushed past him only for Richenda to leap from her seat and throw herself into my arms. 'It is all so horrible,' she wailed.

It took me some time to calm her. Even I understood that this was not a situation that could be helped by the ordering of cake. What do you say to a mother who fears her babies are in danger? I could not imagine her despair. Amy hung around her mother, and every now and then Richenda engulfed her in a huge and tearful hug. That Amy accepted this quietly and without complaint spoke volumes for the mood of those left behind at the hotel room.

I had lost track of Bertram while consoling Richenda, but I spied him coming out of one of the bathrooms. 'Do not go in there, Euphemia,' he said.

It was so unlike Bertram to refer to bathroom functions that I stared like a loon.

'Rory has one of the bellboys in there. Apparently, he was paid to ensure our floor was clear of staff when the kidnapping took place. Rory is in the process of helping him remember all the details of his pay-master.'

'Bellboy,' I said horrified. 'Is he a child?'

'Of course not,' said Bertram. 'Twenty-five, if he is a day. It is a position, not a description of youth.'

'Where is Glanville?' I asked, noticing her absence.

'She went to the police some time ago,' said Richenda. 'We decided not to use the telephone in case the kidnappers had someone on the switchboard listening in. She said she would take a circuitous route so as not to be followed. She is yet to return.'

Bertram and I exchanged worried looks.

'You do not think she has been kidnapped too, do you?' said Richenda in horror.

'Look on the bright side,' said Bertram. 'She could be working with the kidnappers.'

Rory re-entered the room. 'It seems he was only paid to ensure no one stopped the lift at this floor. His pay-master is the butler for this floor. Apparently, he has a reputation among the staff for taking bribes to deliver a wide variety of favours.'

'Where is he?'

'He went off duty a while ago. Apparently, he likes to sup at some inn called The Devil's Lamb. I am going to change and head there.'

'Do you need me?' asked Bertram. 'Only Euphemia and I are not quite finished…'

'No,' said Rory. 'I suspect I will have to beat the truth out of him and that is easier if I do it alone. The bellboy described him as a weaselling sort of a man and a physical coward.'

'What are you doing?' said Richenda.

'Helping,' I said. 'Trust us.'

Richenda turned her red-rimmed and puffy face to me.

'I have no choice,' she said.

'I take it you never telephoned Hans for the same reason,' I said.

'No,' said Richenda quietly.

'Good God,' said Bertram. 'The man has a right to know what is happening with his own children.'

'We have a little time,' I said. 'Why do you not send a telegram from a post office outside the hotel, should one still be open? We cannot fear there will be enemies listening in on the switchboards outside the hotel, that is a level of paranoia even I am not willing to entertain.'

Bertram glanced at his pocket watch. 'I could do that,' he agreed reluctantly. He and Richenda agreed a wording and he left having asked me for the correct change. Rory left to find the butler, leaving the bellboy tied up in one of the bathrooms. Richenda and I wedged the door from outside with a chair. Then I quietly explained to Richenda the next part of my plan but did not reveal the whole circumstances. She opted to help me, saying it would divert her mind until Glanville returned.

When Bertram, nattily attired in his evening suit, walked into Bosenby's, I imagine the last thing he expected to see was his fiancée, sitting on a high stool at the bar, dressed like a tart and sipping champagne. I smiled coquettishly at him. Bertram, if you will excuse the pun, made a beeline for me. He signalled to the bartender to bring us a bottle with such expertise I began to worry.

On the outside Bosenby's looked like the epitome of a gentleman's club. A jolly, wrong-side-of-middle-age porter, with a tolerant smile, welcomed members into the generous lobby. However, as well as yearly membership, it appeared that gentlemen might pay a monthly tariff as long as they were known to be found in what is often crudely referred to as the 'stud book' - Debrett's. It was also possible for members to vouch for guests. I discovered all this when I arrived at the front door earlier in the evening.

''Ello, me darlin',' the porter had said, eyeing me up and down. 'You must be a new girl. Not seen you before. Next time come in by the back gate. Trudi will brief you on the club details.'

I had assumed that I would have to ask for employment, but I did not demur and followed his directions through the London townhouse to a small office in the basement. There, seated behind a desk sat a very smart, elegant, and doubtless once beautiful woman. From her discreet pink-painted lips, to her exquisitely curled (but improbable) red hair, to her tasteful black cocktail dress, she could have passed for a hostess at any smaller country house. When she spoke, it was with carefully rounded vowels.

'I do not know you,' she said bluntly.

Equally bluntly I told her I was new in town and had come hoping for work, and the doorman had directed me straight down to her.

'Stand up,' she said. 'Turn around, slowly. Are you clean?'

'I have no diseases,' I said, biting my inner cheek and hoping the pain would prevent me blushing. 'I also am not fond of alcohol or any other stimulants. Although I will, obviously, indulge with a client if required.'

'Working abroad?' asked the woman.

'In France,' I said, reddening. I knew very little about the country and hoped she would not question me.

'I see,' said Trudi. 'I suppose some gentleman said he would marry you and then left you to work your way home?'

'Something like that,' I said.

'Well, George, the doorman, has a good eye for what our members like. But let me make it clear from the start, this is not a knocking shop. No illegal activity ever takes place here.' I did not manage to mask my surprise for she continued, 'If you want to work somewhere where you can turn several tricks a night I can refer you to a number of places, but our girls do not do that. We are a different kind of establishment. You are rather green, aren't you?'

'Yes,' I said.

'Good. We have a number of members who prefer that. That is why they come here. Several of our girls have left to get married, you know. It all depends. You speak well, and with advice you could... hmm. Anyway. Our members come here to select a mistress. A mistress is a long-term companion, who is available whenever they are in town. All the girls they see here are open to offers. You only accept a gentleman if you wish to. They are looking for companions as much as bed partners, so there must be some chemistry between you. We take a finder's fee that is twenty per cent of what the gentleman offers for your first month of service. After that we take ten percent a month for the next six months and after that five per cent for the rest of the year. Should the arrangement become permanent, as a mistress or a wife, we take one per cent of the initial monthly payment for life. Is that clear enough? We also introduce the gentleman to a lawyer, who will set out the agreement properly. A man's word here is only worth the paper it is signed, sealed and witnessed on. I think you could do rather well. Although you might consider dyeing your hair. Are you interested?'

'Yes, ma'am,' I said. 'That sounds more than fair, and

the best I can hope given my situation.'

'I agree,' said Trudi. 'I will say that unless your contract states you are exclusively to belong to a gentleman, it does not preclude taking another client. We have several girls who manage three or four gentlemen. However, it would be your responsibility to ensure they are all happy with the arrangement. Our lawyer will not suggest an exclusive contract unless you or the gentleman mention it first.'

'It all sounds very business-like,' I said.

'It is. Bosenby's has been running for a very long time. Do I need to say that acting outside our rules, of which you will be given a copy - these can be read to you if you cannot read - incurs a terminal penalty?'

'Of employment?' I said.

'Of life,' said Trudi. She let the threat hang in the air for a moment. 'The one reason we have survived so long is because we adhere to strict rules. Our gentlemen know they are safe coming to us. Before you leave this office, you will sign an agreement that you will never disclose who you see within these walls. And yes, we do keep tabs on our new girls.'

'It is a lot to process,' I said.

Trudi glanced through some papers. 'Go down to the bar. Have a seat and chat to a few gentlemen. There is no-one of significance due in tonight, so you do not have to sign our contract immediately. See if you think this place will suit you. Our gentlemen are of a type.'

I only truly understood what she meant when I realised Bertram was at least ten years younger than any other gentleman in the bar. I began to explain the rules under my breath. Bertram cut me off.

'I couldn't send the wire. Nowhere was open.'

'Do not try to distract me, Bertram! How do you know so much about this place?'

'My father was a member. Tell me, you have not signed anything? I do not fancy having to pay for you for life to the mistress here.'

'Of course not,' I said. 'Although it was touch and go.'

'What exactly are you hoping to accomplish here?'

'What we spoke about earlier. I thought I could talk to the girls.'

'Well, you are here,' said Bertram sighing. 'Let's pray no one recognises you. Whoever would have thought Richenda's dire taste could be useful. Do not even try and persuade me that is not one of her outfits doctored.'

Bertram, less than discreetly, slid me his business card across the bar and then walked off to talk to some of the male members. I finished my drink and, feeling slightly tipsy, I realised I could not remember when I had last eaten. I attempted to mingle with the girls who were out tonight. To my surprise they were friendly and helpful. The majority were also well-educated and intelligent. I surmised more than one story began with a cad of a lover and an angry father. It made me sad, though not that the girls were unhappy. As one explained to me - Amberley, a blonde as fake as her name - 'We are here for the daddies. Older men looking to recapture their youth. If you do not mind an older gentleman, they are not particularly demanding in the physical way but demand a lot of praise and a sort of hero-worship. We are all looking for the right match for us. This is a long game. The right John, I mean gentleman, can set you up for life. Older men are richer, more generous and occasionally their older wives die in childbirth - you need to ensure they never get quite enough away from home if this is your plan - and then they marry you. There are no disapproving parents. No one to stop them. And even if they do not marry you, you are remembered in the will. Usually handsomely. And the family would rather keep the image of the wholesome father than challenge the will - afraid of the scandal, you see. But you do have to be handy with older men, if you get my meaning. It can be quite hard to get the gentleman to stand to attention. The things some of them need you to do! It is better to establish this first.'

'Oh yes,' said a divine brunette, 'I thought I had found the right one until he asked how I felt about him wearing one of my dresses when we - you know. No thank you very much, I said. I'm not that kind of girl.' I almost laughed, but she did not, so I kept a straight face and nodded.

'I do not understand how the guests work,' I said. 'Members can sign other men in?'

'That's for a bit of a look around usually,' said a petite red head with astonishing violet eyes. 'Although some of them ask for contracts that let them lend you out to their friends. No different to working in a brothel if you sign one of those,' she said with a sneer. 'But some girls prefer the variety.'

'I heard that a German delegation was brought in here recently,' I said.

'Oh gosh, yes,' said Amberley. 'What a fuss. Old Porter brought them in. Thinks he's something special, he does. Got the same thing down his trousers as any of the others.'

I bit my cheek again to prevent myself from blushing. Although, I also mused, if I survived this encounter then I would probably never again blush at anything again I might hear in polite society.

'Does he ever lend his mistress out?' I said.

'He's the look but don't touch type,' said Amberley. 'Likes to show off.'

'Is she around? It would be helpful to speak to her. I do not think I want a contract like that, but I would like to enquire how she finds it before I rule it out.'

'Oh, love, did Trudi not explain? Once you find your gentleman, you don't come back here,' said the redhead. 'I mean, why would you? All the action takes place elsewhere.'

'Of course,' I said. 'Do you think she would meet me?'

'Her kind will do anything for money,' said Amberley, 'but she was before our time. We couldn't tell you even if we wanted to. No, love, you stick with the single contract. The gentleman at the bar, I would go exclusive for him for half the normal price. Young and handsome. Can't think why he is here. Let me know if you don't want him and I'll wander over and have a chat.'

'All right,' I said. 'Now I understand better. I will have another talk with him and see what I think. I was looking for an older gentleman really. I am not sure I want it to be a life commitment on my side, if you see what I mean.'

The girls all laughed in a soft, well-trained way and the men in the room all turned their eyes towards us.

'Showtime,' said the little redhead. 'I see one well marked by Father Time. Now to check out his bank roll.' The girls dispersed, and I headed back to my seat at the bar. It was not long before Bertram joined me.

'I will need to bathe a dozen times or more to get the stench of this place off me,' he said.

I smiled. 'I understand,' I said quietly. 'But Porter does have a mistress from here that he likes to show off to his friends. I cannot see how this would cause jealousy as it is his choice.'

'Are you thinking Von Ritter could have made her a better offer?'

'The penalty clauses they invoke here are rather final,' I said.

'Not if you were in Germany,' said Bertram.

'A rich older man, whose older wife is pregnant and may die in childbirth, was described to me as one of the best situations to obtain,' I said.

Bertram shuddered.

'Do not do that. You are meant to like me.'

'Who is she?' asked Bertram.

'The others don't know. Although they do not like Porter.'

'I do not see how this helps us,' said Bertram. 'I will agree it is a damn good motive, but with no proof it is unsubstantiated fiction. It is less than we have on Gottlieb. The arguments between him and Von Klaus may have been the baron refusing to recognise him as a son.'

I nodded. 'I had been struggling to think of why you might kill your benefactor, who was also, unbeknownst to the world, your father, but I suppose if he was not acknowledged he might have become vengeful.'

'Both stories are possible,' said Bertram, 'But we have no proof of either.'

'We could ask Porter's mistress,' I said thoughtfully. 'The girls said she was on contract, so I bet Trudi - the madam here - holds copies in her office.'

'And you know where that is?'

'We could make it look as if we were going to talk to her about my contract but wait until she leaves her office and look through her papers.'

'That sounds simple,' said Bertram with obvious

sarcasm.

'I agree,' I said, rising from my seat and taking his arm. 'Let us do it.'

As Bertram could hardly pull away from me, I towed him down towards the basement. As soon as we were out of earshot from the main bar he began to protest, but I pointed out that we never knew who might be listening around a corner and he quietened. In fact, he adopted a mulish look, which I did not take for refusal, but as a note that he would bring this situation up again and again for the rest of our lives if it happened to go wrong.

For once luck favoured us. We arrived to catch sight of Trudi leaving her office. 'She will have locked it,' whispered Bertram in my ear. His sideburns tickled me, and I barely held back a giggle. Perhaps I had imbibed more champagne than I realised. The taste had been sweetly apple-like and the bubbles had popped on my tongue in the most delightful manner that I have given no real though to the fact that it was alcohol, something I rarely indulged in.

'Go try it,' I asked as Trudi disappeared. 'We might be in luck. I'll watch in the corridor.'

'Make a sound like an owl if anyone is coming,' said Bertram.

'Why would there be an owl...' I began, but he had already gone.

It took him perhaps a few minutes to find, open and remove the contract we required, but standing in the corridor alone time passed with painful slowness. My stomach churned like a whirlpool with anxiety. The lack of food and addition of alcohol began to make me nauseous. The feeling intensified to the degree that I began to look around for a plant pot or bucket. My upbringing would not allow me to vomit on a carpet. In fact, I doubt whether my mother ever vomited in her life. I, it appeared, was not made of such stern stuff. I could not move for more than a few feet from my post and there appeared to be no available receptacle. My need had increased to an intolerable level. I could only pray that no one would find Bertram. I retreated out of sight to a window we had passed earlier.

Fortunately, it was not barred as many basement windows are, but it had been painted shut more than once. However, with the use of my shoe I managed to batter the latch until it opened. Then with a supreme effort of strength that only blind panic could procure I hauled up the sash and stuck my head out. The window opened onto a back alley and not the busy street. The window was higher than I might have imagined, being around six to seven feet above the ground. A large striped tom eyed me curiously. I thanked God for the discreetness of the location and vomited copiously onto the ground. I immediately felt better, but the sensation did not last. Wave after wave of stomach pain and nausea resulted in my repeating such an unladylike action, and a heartfelt promise never to drink champagne again.[8]

Eventually I was wrung dry. I leant over the ledge, feeling the fresh air against my face. The cat had disappeared, and I feared it might have been the victim of my inaccurate aim. At that moment I felt King and Country could quite frankly go hang - as well as many a German and diplomat who had got themselves mixed up in this ruckus. All I wanted was to go and lie in a darkened room with a cool, damp cloth on my forehead. I was in the

---

[8]A resolution I have kept to this day.

midst of imaging such a state of joy when Bertram erupted from around the corner. I knew it was him without looking as he yelled, 'Emergency! She's coming!'

I stepped back from the window and saw him approaching, jacket tails flapping in the wind and a piece of paper clutched in one hand.

'The window!' he cried. 'How inspired!' And before I could object he leapt through it more nimbly than I ever imagined he could and was gone. 'I'll catch you,' he cried a moment before I heard the shriek and thump that accompanied him discovering why I had actually opened the window.

However, I could not stop and explain, for behind me in the corridor I heard the clip-clop of a lady's shoes approaching. This was also accompanied by a lung bursting shout of 'George! George! Don't let the buggers get away.' I barely had time to wonder if half the men in London were called George.

I pulled myself up onto the window ledge. Gentlemen may be able to leap through windows like fawns, but skirts are no lady's friend in such an endeavour. Below me I saw that Bertram had skidded through that which should never be mentioned by a lady, and he had fallen on his posterior. This had inevitably smeared the unnameable matter even further along the ground outside. I looked around. The cat now sat on the ledge of a window opposite. It groomed its paw and smirked, as much as a cat can smirk, at my predicament.

I bundled up my skirts and jumped. Bertram gallantly made his way towards me. He would have to throw those shoes out. However, instead of my coming nicely to rest in his arms, I hovered in mid-air for a moment. I saw his eyes roll up in astonishment. Then there came a ripping noise as my skirts, which had momentarily got caught on the latch, came free and I landed heavily on Bertram, who landed heavily on the floor. It was by far and away the most unpleasant embrace of our careers.

We scrambled to our feet, became even dirtier in the process, and we ran. I found it surprisingly easy to run, and surprisingly cold. Then I looked down and realised that no one in London would recognise me from this escapade. They would not be looking at my face. I had, indeed, left most of my skirts dangling off the latch.

Bertram caught sight of me askance and his mouth gaped in shock.

'A cab,' I panted as I ran alongside him. 'Give me your jacket and hail us a cab.'

For once Bertram did not argue with me and so it was that we found ourselves in the most expensive cab journey I can to this day recall; Bertram in shirt sleeves unable to speak at the dreadfulness of it all, I with his jacket wrapped around my bare legs, and both us stinking more than any fish head the alleyway cat might devour that night.

Chapter Fourteen
Matters Move on Apace

Having been a servant myself leaves one with a sixth sense of where a servant's entrance can usually be located. By the time we had climbed the stairs to our hotel suite we were both exhausted. Bertram's face had acquired a greenish tinge, which I hoped had nothing to do with the exertion. Both of us paid no heed to who else was in the suite but bolted for bathrooms. Unfortunately, Bertram first tried the one where Rory had been keeping the bellboy, who cried out in dismay, doubtless thinking this was some new and unusual form of torture.

I stripped off my rags and plunged into the bath before the fancy taps had barely made an impression on the water level. I expected Richenda to enter at any moment shouting and demanding to know what had happened, but she did not do so. A soft knock came on the door as I began to scrub at my skin, and Rory's voice called, 'Are you alright, Euphemia?'

'I need to bathe,' I called back. 'But I am unhurt.' Having fallen on Bertram I did not even appear to have a single bruise.

'Hurry yourself,' said Rory. 'Things are moving apace out here. There will be time for ablutions later.'

I realised that to call through the bathroom door he must have entered my bedroom. This is not something a man who has trained as a butler does lightly. I finished as soon as I could and bundled myself into towels. Then I opened my closet and scanned my clothes for something I could dress in without a maid and which would take less than an hour of effort. Glanville! Surely she was back by now! I called for her to attend to me as I pulled fresh under linen from a drawer. Not a stitch of what I had worn earlier would ever touch my skin again.

The door opened, and I almost fainted on the spot.

'Merry!' I cried, dropping my things and my towel as I flung myself into her arms. 'You are back. All is well.'

Merry returned my embrace firmly. 'I am afraid not,' she said. I could tell at once from her voice that she had been crying.

'What has happened,' I said stepping back. 'Tell me that it is not…'

'No, not that,' said Merry. 'Let us get you into some clothes before you take a chill and we can discuss matters with the gentlemen.' She gave a small sob as she rescued a stocking from the ground and held it out to me.

Merry helped me dress in silence. A lady's clothes require attention and skill to put on, and the act is not helped when the lady in question is damp, distressed and her hair has come down. However, in a most reasonable space of time I was presentable enough to join the rest of the company. I entered with Merry on my arm, paler and frailer than I had ever seen her.

Bertram was slumped in a chair. His hair was wet and had begun to curl. He had not bothered with his customary pomade. I had no idea that his hair was naturally wavy, and this distracted me for a moment. Rory paced past me. 'You took your time,' he said.

I blinked and sat down in a chair myself. All the physical activity of the day suddenly caught up with me. I must have paled significantly as Rory modified his tone. 'Bertram has caught me up with your activities.'

'There is a name?' I asked Bertram.

'And an address,' he replied. 'We shall go there shortly, but...' he looked at Merry. 'Richenda has gone to pay the ransom. Merry was sent back as a sign of good faith, but Glanville is still not yet returned. Richenda, despite Rory's protests, has taken this all upon herself.' He swallowed. 'She can draw the money herself. She has shares in the Stapleford bank.'

'But the amount was impossible,' I said.

'Rory got them to see sense. It appears they are most keen to be rid of their charges and accepted a reduced payment on the condition Richenda went alone.'

'I would have followed her,' said Rory, 'but Merry was in no state to be left alone with Amy. I did not feel... and you were... and I did not know if you might...' He sat down and put his head in his hands. 'I should have gone.'

Bertram went over and awkwardly patted his back. 'Nothing you could do, old man. If these chaps are as nasty as Merry says...' he looked over at me. 'They made Merry hold a cat while they killed it, that's how they got blood on her dress. She was blindfolded, and the cat was swaddled.'

'I thought it was one of the babies,' said Merry faintly. 'They took off the blindfold because I would not stop screaming. When I saw it was a cat they laughed in my face.' I swallowed, for the first time grateful that I had no bile left to spill.

'If you had gone with Richenda,' continued Bertram, 'I would not put it past them to have killed the babies on the spot.'

'Aye, mebbe,' said Rory, but he raised his head out of his hands. 'But what's to do?'

'Merry, what can you remember of where you were?' I

193

asked. Merry leant against the wall and mutedly shook her head.

'They kept her blindfolded on the way there,' said Rory. 'And when they did take it off, the place was kept very dark. They tied her to a pipe with a length of rope just long enough that she could tend to the babies.'

'Did they say anything that might help?' I asked Merry. 'Anything at all?'

Again Merry shook her head. She seemed almost in a daze and I began to fear they had harmed her in other ways.

'From what Merry remembers,' said Rory, 'it appears they spoke German.'

'Those bloody Huns!' said Bertram. 'It's all of a piece. They are devils.'

I struggled for words. Bertram, now in a fit of passion, made little sense. His wits had flown away on a tide of anger. Rory sat grim and despairing, while my poor Merry was a pale shadow of herself. I could not think of what to do.

I knew that we must hurry to the house of Porter's mistress and see if there was any truth in our idea she was involved with Klaus Von Ritter and that this evidence must be discovered before breakfast tomorrow or we risked sending an innocent man to the gallows. But how could we leave Merry and Rory? How could we abandon Richenda and her babies? I could call Hans. I strongly doubted Richenda had called him even now. But how could he aid us being so far away? An idea crept up on me and I was trying so hard not to look it full in the face. I looked over at Bertram, who had paused mid-rant. His complexion had become ashen and I knew he had had the same thought.

'If this is Richard's plan -' he began.

'Do not say it,' I begged. 'There is nothing we can do.'

But Bertram would not shy away from the real awfulness. 'If it is,' he said, 'then now he has the babies and Richenda. All that stands between him and the ownership of Stapleford Hall. Hans would have no claim and Amy is adopted. He may have hoped to capture her too in the first instance, but now Richenda alone and the babies is as good a bargain as he can hope for.'

I nodded miserably.

'Dear God,' Merry spoke for the first time, her words like ice through my heart. 'He means to kill them all.'

I turned away and choking back the tears that threatened to engulf me, I made for my bedroom. Richenda and her children were in mortal danger somewhere in the metropolis and we had no idea where they were.

'Did she not even give you a hint of where she was going?' begged Bertram to Rory.

'She said only that the voice on the telephone line made her swear on the lives of her children she would say nothing.'

'She would need to get a cab,' said Bertram. 'Have you tried to find out which she took, or where it went?'

Rory nodded, 'And I've paid several boys to keep enquiring. Nothing yet.'

'The butler,' I said, pivoting on my heel, 'The one at the inn. What did he have to share?'

'I left him unconscious,' said Rory. 'Whoever hired him scared him more than a beating at my hands.'

'Where is he now?' said Bertram.

Rory shrugged hopelessly. 'I didnae try and lug him back. I thought... there had been no telephone call... I didnae know…'

At this moment the air shattered with the ringing of the telephone apparatus. All of us froze. The bell rang three times. I picked up my skirts and ran for it.

'Yes,' I yelled into the mouth piece. 'What?'

Michael's voice came on the line. 'Euphemia?'

'Oh, thank God. I thought you were the kidnappers,' I said. 'They have Richenda and the babies. They are going to kill them.'

Michael hesitated for a mere second. 'Do you know who killed Von Ritter?'

'No, you beastly man, and I don't care,' I cried. 'Did you not hear what I said!' And I broke into heavy, ugly sobs. Through them I heard the sound of a muttered conversation on the other end of the line with Michael saying, 'Hysterical. No idea.' Then a different voice spoke on the line. 'Euphemia?'

'Fitzroy! Eric! Oh, thank God.' I began half laughing, half crying.

The others crowded around me, and I felt Bertram's hand on my back. I took strength from it. 'Eric, we need your help. We believe Richard to be behind the kidnapping and he has tricked Richenda into going to him alone. It is all about that wretched will and Stapleford Hall.'

'I am aware,' said Fitzroy. 'Now, Euphemia, I need you to take yourself in hand.' Then with surprising gentleness and a professional thoroughness that showed the logical working of his mind, he had me take him through the events of today.

'What do I do?' I asked him.

'You continue with the task entrusted to you, to discover who killed Von Ritter. The lives of millions rest on your actions. You must go to this woman and see if your theory holds up.'

'But -' I began.

'My dear girl,' said Fitzroy, 'I do not ask this because I am a callous man, but because I am unable to do this myself. Michael and I will be engaged for a while longer here. I cannot tell you any more, but I do not take your despair lightly. I am truly sorry, but you have a duty as a subject of the British Empire to serve your King and Country.' I could feel tears rolling down my face. Fitzroy continued, 'The lives of thousands, all of them fathers and sons, rest on how you deal with the situation with the delegation. If it is possible a member of the British diplomatic service is at fault and we do not find this out first, the results will be catastrophic.'

It was at this moment that the final piece fell into place in my mind. Porter, described by more than one as wanting to be the centre of attention; a man who was rising in power due to his determination of will and his belief in himself; his belief that he was better than anyone else; who thought the world revolved around him. How might such a man take the stealing of his mistress?

I swallowed. 'Is there anything you can do?' I said.

'Perhaps,' said Fitzroy. 'Let us hope we have a little time on our side. If I can discover where Merry was taken then you, or even I, may be able to get there in time.'

'But she was blindfolded,' I said.

'I know,' said Fitzroy, 'But she has her other senses. You have always spoken of her as a smart girl. If she is prepared to be questioned closely I may be able to narrow down where they are. But it will take time. I can spend the time if I remain where I am. I cannot leave. You must continue your investigation. By the time you have your results I will hope to have something for you.' He paused and then said with a sincerity rarely heard in his voice. 'I cannot promise anything, Euphemia, but I will do my best.'

'Thank you,' I said and passed the listening piece to Merry. 'He needs to talk to you. You can trust him. I believe he is our only chance.' Then I fetched my coat. 'Come, Bertram, we have a woman to interview.' I left Rory staring after us. Further explanations could wait. Time was not on our side.

Of course, in the carriage, Bertram made me tell him all, but we had time even as the horses sped through the night to the address written on the contract. He listened and to my surprise did not react in anger. 'I see what he is trying to do. It is a long shot, but I think the better of him for trying.'

'Where could he be that he cannot leave?' I said.

Bertram rubbed his temples with his fingers. 'I gave that some thought while you spoke with him and I remembered that he said something about the King meeting the delegation? That it was a spur of the moment thing?'

I nodded. Realisation dawned. 'Do you think he is with HIM?' I said in awe.

'I suspect, and I have no doubt he will never reveal this to us, but I suspect that he and the King were on the way to the Exhibition in a discreet manner when the news of Von Ritter reached them.'

'So, he is hiding the King until this all blows over?'

'That is my guess,' said Bertram.

'Where?' I said. My curiosity in that moment blotting out everything else. 'Where do you hide a king in times of trouble or potential trouble?'

'Somewhere we could not even hazard to guess,' said Bertram. 'And we should keep it that way.'

The cab pulled up outside a neat block of flats opposite a small French restaurant. Bertram got out and paid the driver. Then he took my arm and walked across the road. 'I think we can trust the neighbourhood.'

'Bertram, we do not have time,' I protested.

'When did you last eat anything? We cannot keep going without food. We can spare half an hour for some light refreshment. I do not think we will be seeing much sleep this night.'

I sighed. 'Half an hour then. You will have to tip the waiter more than normal for speedy service.'

'Err, Euphemia, about that,' said Bertram. 'After paying the cabbie I do not have...'

I smiled for the first time in what felt like a very long time. 'I will pay, Bertram. You can take me to dinner tomorrow when we are celebrating.'

So, although my mother would have disapproved most strongly, I bought us both a simple, but nourishing supper of soup, fish and *iles flottantes*. I suppose, in hindsight, it could have been thought of as akin to nursery or invalid food, but we both enjoyed it immensely. Bertram huffed a little when I skipped the meat course, but I did not waver in my resolve.

Although we stuck to our time limit, by the time we left, the sky had turned that dark purple velvet colour that only appears above the intense light thrown by city lamps. The street was quiet enough that I could pause in the middle of the road and look up at the stars.

'Makes you feel a bit small, does it not?' said Bertram. 'That as specks within God's great creation, we and our troubles are insignificant.'

I shook my head. 'No, night sky never fails to make me feel blessed that I am a part of this, no matter how small. Do you not feel blessed to see and be part of such beauty?'

Bertram's rather romantic response almost caused us to be run down by a carriage.

We were let into the flats by the doorman, who seemed to think nothing of visitors arriving at all times of the day and night. Fortunately, the contract was detailed enough to name the flat number, but he did not even trouble to ask us.

'We must look respectable,' said Bertram.

'Or just unrespectable enough,' I said. 'Maybe he saw us kissing outside.'

'Good heavens, but then he would think that you… that I… I must set him right at once,' said Bertram. It took me a little effort to prevent him from doing so.

'We are not meant to be drawing attention to ourselves,' I said.

We knocked on the door of apartment 4A. I admit I expected it to be neat and functional, but I was unprepared for the lavish sight that met our eyes when the door opened. A neat little maid, scarcely thirteen years of age, opened the door. Behind her I saw the long narrow hall was hung with white silk and a luscious Chinese rug that ran the length of the hallway. Two prints hung, one each side of the hallway. They were both clearly Old Masters, but their subject was not one that was normally seen in the drawing room and left no doubt of the occupation of the lady owner of this place. Bertram coloured beetroot on seeing them.

'Is Miss Anderson at home?' I enquired.

The little maid bobbed. 'It is late, madam, but I can see. Who shall I say is calling?'

I decided to get right to the nub of the issue. 'Please tell her it is friends of Baron Von Ritter.'

The maid looked as if she would have asked our names, but I interrupted her. 'Perhaps there is a room where we may wait while you enquire? We can hardly stand on the doorstep, can we?'

This had been what she clearly intended us to do, but I looked down my nose the way my mother has taught me. She is less than five feet tall but can make a Duke cry with one sharp sentence - or so she claims to have done in her youth. Though she has never told me what the Duke did to earn such a rebuke.

The maid took us into a small ante-room. It too was white, but this time there was a profusion of mirrors on the walls. Candles with crystals hung around them were strewn around two white painted tables in what I presume was meant to be the French style. There was also a plumply padded chaise longue, on which sat a riding crop, and a pair of leather armchairs. Unaccountably the room made me feel uncomfortable.

'I do not like this,' I said.

'It is exactly the kind of place where a certain kind of lady would entertain,' said Bertram. 'Let us stay standing.'

I forbore asking him how he knew this because an amazingly beautiful woman had entered the room. She was of moderate height and build, but her skin was porcelain white, her long, free-flowing hair darker than a raven's wing, and her eyes the colour of jade. She wore a shimmery silver silk gown and, I would have laid money, nothing else. Beside me Bertram caught his breath and then tried to change it into a cough. I ignored him.

'I do not believe we have been introduced,' said Miss Anderson in a well-modulated voice that barely hinted at her background.

'I am sorry to tell you that Baron Von Ritter is dead.'

She sank dramatically down onto the chaise longue and actually uttered the words, 'You lie!'

'I am afraid not,' said Bertram. 'He was taken ill at the exhibition at Crystal Palace and passed away.'

Miss Anderson sat up. I thought I saw a calculating look in her eyes, but it was gone in a moment. 'Poor Algernon,' she said. 'It will have ruined all his plans. Did he send you to tell me? We were to meet tomorrow at six p.m. at the Chelsea tea rooms. He must be dreadfully upset. It is all too tragic, though I hardly knew him, of course.'

Bertram threw me a confused looked. 'I say, I thought when we mentioned his name you came over all distressed.'

'I am extremely compassionate,' said Miss Anderson.

'I expect you were glorious on stage,' I said.

Miss Anderson rounded on me. 'Look, what d'you want?' she asked, her accent beginning to slip. 'Does Algernon need me to go to him?'

'Would he normally send a couple to escort you?' I asked.

'Not like you two, he wouldn't. What's going on?'

I eyed her up. Bertram seemed baffled, but I recognised a businesswoman in Miss Anderson. 'I think it might be helpful if we all laid our cards on the table. We believe the Baron was murdered. Would I be right in thinking he had asked you to go to Germany with him?'

'How is this any of your business?' snapped the woman.

'I only want the truth. Whatever that may be,' I said. 'Tell me the truth and I will hand over your contract from

Bosenby's to do with as you wish. You can keep the contract, or you can tear it into bits and break with Porter.'

Miss Anderson tilted her head to one side. 'I'll tell you whatever you want if you have that to bargain with.'

Bertram took it from his pocket. Miss Anderson made a grab for it, but I intercepted her. 'I do not want to be told a fairy story, Miss Anderson. I want the truth and only the truth. If I cannot confirm your story, you will not get your piece of paper.'

'And how are you going to confirm it?' said Miss Anderson. 'If he is dead and there is no one to confirm it?'

'Friedrich Gottlieb,' I said.

Miss Anderson shot to her feet. 'If I told Klaus once I told him a thousand times, that good-for-nothing son of his was after his money. Why else should he care about Klaus and me? It's not as if Klaus is cheating on *his* mother, seeing as he comes from the wrong side of the blanket anyway.'

'Interesting,' murmured Bertram.

'Your relationship with Porter and Ritter,' I said. 'Please clarify.'

Miss Anderson moved to an armchair and opened up a hidden panel. She took out a cigarette and asked Bertram for a light. 'I do not smoke, madam,' he said. 'Please answer my lady's question.'

Miss Anderson pulled a cruel and mocking face for a moment. She lit the cigarette herself and inhaled. She closed her eyes and exhaled. Finally, she spoke. 'All right, if I am to come clean I might as well tell you the whole lot. Porter is a nice enough gent. On the rise in the right circles.'

'About to drop you, was he?' said Bertram.

'Not at all,' said Miss Anderson. 'He likes things tidy.

His wife is for making the children. I'm for entertainment. Those are his words, not mine. Only it isn't very enter-bloody-taining for me.' Her eyes glazed slightly as she took on a reflective tone. 'He provides well, but he likes things done a certain way.'

'I don't think we need to hear,' said Bertram.

'It's all right,' said Miss Anderson, 'I don't kiss and tell. Let's just say that when you're going through the same performance for the hundredth time and you find yourself wondering if the fish you have in the kitchen will stretch to another day, then the excitement of the adventure is on the wane.' She stubbed out her cigarette in a small silver ash tray and stood up. 'Don't you get it? He was no bleedin' fun. And there was I, tied to him with that dreadful contract for the rest of my natural life. Of course, I broached the matter, but Algie doesn't like change, does he?' She ran her hands over her forearms. 'He come on a bit rough, if you know what I mean. Left me in no doubt that what is his, is his for life.'

'So, Von Ritter was your way out?'

Miss Anderson wrinkled her nose and to my surprise gave a little sniff. 'I suppose that is what I thought at first, but he was a good bloke, Klaus. He liked a laugh and he knew how to treat a lady. The real laugh is Porter took me to meet him at Bosenby's to show off. "Look what I have." Very much his style. But someone turned up that he had to talk to and I was left with Klaus.'

'You made your plans in one night?' said Bertram. 'That seems like too much of a fairy tale to me.'

'This was months ago. Klaus has been in and out of the country on business and well, he and I, we took up with one another. I explained it was against my agreement, but he seemed a harmless old man. I didn't think he would actually want to do - you know.' she jerked her head. 'Boy, was I to learn not to judge a book by its appearance. Klaus was a right Casanova, I can tell you. He knew how to please women, that man. Said he'd had a lot of practice. But that wasn't it, and you can call me a liar to my face if you want, but I liked him. We had fun together, and when he suggested I might enjoy myself in Germany being with him, and I thought about it compared to my life with Algie - well, the choice was obvious. And now the poor old blighter's gone and died. I hope it was a disgraceful exit.' She gave us a watery smile. 'That's what he would have wanted.'

'Actually, we think he was murdered,' I said.

'By Porter,' said Bertram helpfully.

It took us almost an hour to calm down her hysterics, but by the end we were both convinced that she had intended to run off with Von Ritter and that it would fit with Porter's character for him to act vengefully. In the privacy of her bedroom she showed me the remains of bruises that Porter had inflicted on her when he had recently accused her of flirting. All of them were carefully positioned not to be on show during normal daywear and all of them looked to have been very painful. When we explained what we needed her to do she was almost eager.

Chapter Fifteen
Midnight Manoeuvres

Catching a cab in the metropolis in the middle of the night is not as easy as you might think. Getting past the doorman at the hotel where a diplomatic delegation is staying is almost impossible. Fortunately, the officer we had spoken to at Crystal Palace had drawn the short straw and was on night duty. Under our direction he gathered the remainder of the delegation in the deserted downstairs lobby. I took the precaution of getting the increasingly curious doorman to lock the exits.

Dietrich Habermann came down first. I could have believed he had stepped out of his office only minutes before. He wore his well-pressed suit and not a trace of sleep showed about his face although, by now, we were nearing midnight. He bowed to us both. 'I assume this is a matter of some import?' he said politely.

Bertram assented and asked him to sit. He did so, crossing his legs with careful precision. Friedrich Gottlieb came down next in a flannel green dressing gown that showed glimpses of striped pyjamas beneath. He was not happy. Only the presence of the police encouraged him to stay.

Robert Draper came down in the suit he had worn earlier that day. His shirt was undone, and he smelled of alcohol. He fell into rather than sat on one of the grouped chairs.

Rudolf Beiersdorf arrived next. His white hair stood on end. He had thrown a coat over his sleeping attire and appeared confused. 'Is there a fire?' he asked. When assured not, he sat down but continued to look bewildered.

Algernon Porter came down last. I should have expected this. He had taken the time to dress and even shave. He looked every inch the statesman. Or he did until he saw Miss Anderson. At this point he asked in a stern tone, 'What is this meaning of this?'

Miss Anderson took this as a cue and flew at him screaming about him destroying all her chances. As neither Bertram or I had had any indication she would do anything of the sort we were quite caught off-guard. Happily, there were enough police to intervene. With the contract as evidence against him, Porter could not deny knowing Miss Anderson. And her crude scathing criticism of him and his peccadilloes stirred him in ways a police interrogation could not have done. Within half an hour he was a broken man and had confessed everything. When we left, Miss Anderson was being comforted by Friedrich Gottlieb, whom we overheard saying how he had misjudged her and that she had obviously cared deeply for Klaus. I took a step towards him, but Bertram put a restraining hand on my arm. He went over to them and carefully put the contract beside her on the arm rest. She affected not to notice, but by the time he returned to me it had made its way into her pocket.

Outside the hotel, I asked Bertram, 'Should we go back inside and ring up the hotel, or shall we take a cab?'

'Cab,' said Bertram firmly. 'They will either be waiting for Fitzroy to call them or be embarked on a rescue. Either way, if we ring them up we will merely delay them.'

'I am not sure I have enough money,' I said, rummaging in my purse.

'We will tell the doorman to put it on our bill,' said

Bertram stoutly. He hailed a cab and then promised the man double, no, triple the fare if he could get us there quickly. We fairly flew through the night. My heart was in my mouth. We had solved Fitzroy's mystery, but had he come through for us in return? Bertram gripped my hand. 'Whatever happens,' he said. 'I am ready.' I was not sure if he was telling me or himself.

'Bertram,' I asked trying to distract us both, 'why did you stop carrying change?'

Bertram looked a little surprised. 'You said you did not like me fiddling with the coins in my pockets. You were quite forceful about it.'

'Couldn't you have coins and not fiddle?'

'No, dear,' said Bertram. 'No man can resist fiddling with his pocket change.'

At the Carlton we left a distressed doorman and angry cabbie behind us and ran for the elevator. 'It might get rather rough, you know,' said Bertram. 'I am not sure you should come on any rescue.'

I bridled but decided to argue the point when I knew what was coming next. Bertram threw open the broken door to the suite and we heard the sound of babies crying. I sprinted forward and found Richenda, tired and dirty, sitting on the settle clinging to her children. 'I will never leave you again,' she was saying to the squalling children.

'Are they hurt?' I cried running forward. Merry intercepted me.

'Only tired and hungry. It's been a long night.'

'So, did you find my murderer?' I whirled to find Fitzroy leaning against a wall, smoking a cigar.

'Algernon Porter,' said Bertram.

'Damn it,' said Fitzroy. 'That will cause a stink.' To his

credit he did not ask us if we were sure.

'But how did you…?' I asked.

'Merry has an excellent memory,' said Fitzroy. 'After she had gone through all the details no more than twenty times I managed to locate the most likely of two probable sites. I could not go myself, so I sent men in. As you can see they were successful.'

'The kidnappers?' said Bertram.

'Were not the priority. My men had orders to rescue the children. I imagine the kidnappers saw the overwhelming force and decided that retreat was the better part of valour.' said Fitzroy. 'Funny thing is, I have just had a wire saying that two German nationals, who had been marked as persons of interest by officials, have been found dead on the Old Kent Road. Shot, would you believe?'

'Did you…?' I asked him.

Fitzroy pretended to take offence. Then he smiled. 'No. I don't leave a mess behind me and neither do my people. I rather think it was a message for you, Richenda.'

At this point, Richenda looked up and stopped talking to the children. Merry took the opportunity to sweep in and take them off to bed. 'For me?' said Richenda.

'Doubtless your charming brother ordered their execution for messing up. In fact, I am not entirely sure that they were not trying to double-cross him and take the money for themselves. Either way, they would have killed you all if my people had not arrived in the nick of time.'

Richenda paled. 'It is not that I am not grateful,' she said turning to me, 'but who is this extraordinary individual?'

Fitzroy gave a crack of laughter. 'I am a good friend of Bertram and Euphemia, ma'am, and your good servant.' He swept an extravagant bow. Then he turned to us.

'Bertie, Effie, good job. I cannot say we have stopped the war, but with luck and honesty you may have held it back another few months. Your country thanks you.' He gave another crack of laughter and walked out.

'The strange people you two know,' said Richenda in a disapproving voice.

'Ma'am?' called a faint voice. Richenda's lady's maid stood in the doorway. She looked as if she had fought a dozen hedges and lost.

'Good heavens, Glanville. We had quite forgot all about you with all this business. Where have you been?'

'I got caught up in a suffragette march, ma'am. I was arrested and thrown into jail…'

Bertram and I did not hear the rest of her story for we were laughing too hard. Attracted by the noise, Rory came out of his room, took one look at the chaos around him then, pulling his best butler face, retreated back into his room and closed the door.

The End

The Euphemia Martins Mysteries Series

A Death in the Family

A Death in the Highlands

A Death in the Asylum

A Death in the Wedding Party

A Death in the Pavilion

A Death in the Loch

A Death for Kind and Country

A Death for a Cause

A Death by Arson

A Death Overseas

Proudly published by Accent Press

www.accentpress.co.uk

Lightning Source UK Ltd.
Milton Keynes UK
UKHW042329200119
335915UK00001B/11/P